THE COLOUR OF VIOLENCE

George Armitage was only a moderately
successful author, but he lived the kind of
quiet life he wanted to. His wife would have
preferred   more   luxury   and   was
discontented with the way things were.
Then, because he had been told that his
writing showed that he didn't know what
violence was really like, Armitage went out
to view the scene of a murder at a motorway
under construction. This seemingly minor
act was to have a shattering effect on him
and all those about him as they became
swept up in the violence that accompanied a
daring bank robbery . . .

THE COLOUR OF VIOLENCE

Jeffrey Ashford

ATLANTIC LARGE PRINT
Chivers Press, Bath, England.
Curley   Publishing,   Inc.,
South Yarmouth, Mass., USA.

Library of Congress Cataloging-in-Publication Data

Ashford, Jeffrey, 1926—
   The colour of violence / Jeffrey Ashford.
     p. cm.—(Atlantic large print)
   ISBN 0–7927–0452–5 (lg.print)
   1. Large type books. I. Title.
[PR6060.E43C65   1991]   90–44950
823′.914—dc20   CIP

British Library Cataloguing in Publication Data

Ashford, Jeffrey 1926—
   The colour of violence.
   Rn: Roderic Jeffries I. Title
   823.914 [F]

   ISBN 0–7451–9976–3
   ISBN 0–7451–9987–9 pbk

This Large Print edition is published by Chivers Press, England, and Curley Publishing, Inc, U.S.A. 1991

Published by arrangement with the author

U.K. Hardback ISBN   0 7451 9976 3
U.K. Softback ISBN   0 7451 9987 9
U.S.A. Softback ISBN   0 7927 0452 5

THE COLOUR OF VIOLENCE

CHAPTER ONE

In the bedroom of their rented cottage, George Armitage tried for the third time to force the bottom half of the collar stud through the holes in the neckband of his stiff fronted shirt and wing collar. The stud tilted and fell down inside his shirt. 'Hell!' he said, exasperated.

Gwen, his wife, spoke sharply. 'Do hurry up, we're late as it is.'

'The later the better.' He tried to reach down inside the shirt for the stud.

She looked away from the mirror. 'If only you'd done as I wanted and bought a decent set of tails. As it is ...' She stopped, nibbled her lower lip for a second, her expression of annoyance deepening the lines about her face, then turned back to lipstick her lips.

He found the bottom half of the stud. He attacked the shirt and collar again.

'George,' she said, 'you won't talk stupidly tonight, will you?'

He grunted, as the now secured collar and shirt dug into his neck. Either he was getting fatter or everything had shrunk.

'You know what I mean, don't you?' she persisted. 'It's not at all funny or clever, even though you seem to think it is.' She removed the silk scarf she'd used to protect her

1

petticoat, went past the bed and slipped into the ice-blue, full skirted, long-sleeved evening dress she'd bought two days before. 'All you manage to do is upset people. You know why you talk like that, don't you? It's simply because you're jealous.'

'I suppose so,' he agreed. In fact, he wasn't jealous of anyone, but he couldn't persuade her that all he was doing was pulling the legs of some of the rich and famous of Ethington to discover how much sense of humour they had left.

'Then, just for once, swallow your jealousy.'

He studied her. At thirty-six, after nine years of marriage, she had physically altered very little. She had a good figure, as yet only lightly touched by the bulges of age, and always took a great deal of care over her appearance. Yet what she had lost was the fresh pleasure of her youth and in its place she had developed a general discontent, so often shown by the petulant set of her mouth. But she had only to laugh, to be gay, and she irresistibly reminded him of how she'd been when they'd married. 'That dress really suits you,' he said, thinking the words would please her.

'D'you think so?' She smoothed the front down with the palm of her right hand and turned to look once more at her reflection in the wardrobe mirror. 'I wish,' she said slowly, 'I'd bought that other dress.'

He felt a quick stab of annoyance that was reflected in his tone of voice when he said: 'You mean the one we couldn't afford even more than we couldn't afford this one?'

'It was more *soigné*.'

He began to tie his white tie, a task that very soon had him swearing. By the time the night was over, it would have cost at least twenty-five pounds and he wasn't even going to enjoy it. Why wasn't one, in this day and age, allowed to wear casual clothes to a hunt ball: what was a hunt ball doing in this day and age?

'For pity's sake, George, get a move on or we'll only arrive in time for "The Queen".'

'I can't get the tie to work.'

'You really are fumble-fisted.' She tied the tie without any trouble.

Their car, an ancient and rusting Hillman, refused to start. He tried the choke in and the choke out, the accelerator down on the floorboards and the accelerator untouched. The battery audibly began to weaken.

'This car!' she said, in tones of hatred.

'There's only one thing left—a belt on the dashboard.' He hit the dashboard with his clenched fist and then turned the ignition key once more. The starter engaged and the engine fired. He laughed. 'The oldest trick in the mechanic's handbook and it seldom fails.'

'You've just got to buy another car,' she

3

snapped.

He was about to answer that he'd ordered a Rolls only the day before, but restrained himself. Whereas he managed to find a wry amusement in many of their minor troubles, she usually found only angry annoyance.

★   ★   ★

The rectangular recreation room was sixty feet long, thirty wide, and fifteen high, with windows along three walls. Prisoners usually spent two hours a day in it, except at week-ends when there were not sufficient warders on duty, and there was a wide choice of games ranging from table tennis to chess, television, radio, and a large assortment of newspapers and magazines, but it was most popular as a clearing house for information, a market for tobacco, and a betting shop.

By tradition, started no one knew when but zealously guarded, the clock end of the recreation room was reserved for the Big Men: top mobsters, and snout barons, and the occasional loner whose character or career commanded unusual respect. As with any stable social system, those at the bottom longed to be seen to be friendly with those at the top, while those at the top were conscious of their superiority. Healey was a poor fish, weedy in appearance, very excitable by nature, who longed to ingratiate himself with the aristocracy and who seemed immune to snubs, insults, or even open threats of violence. He was always as near as possible to the carefully arranged tables at the clock end, ready to do anything that was demanded of him and even occasionally daring to join in conversations. To some, he became a jester, ready to be the butt of cruel practical jokes.

He edged his way to a table at which sat two men, listened to what they were saying, and then joined in. 'Wouldn't you reckon a hundred grand made for a big job, Lofty?'

Weir ignored the question.

Healey persevered. 'What about you, Wally? Don't you reckon a hundred makes any job a top one?'

'Belt up,' muttered Farnes. He was a huge man and his strength was staggering. He'd once run amuck in another prison and it had taken five warders to overpower him: three of them had had to be taken off to hospital.

'Of course, I'm talking about a hundred grand to each member of the mob.' He made a careful point of using prison slang, but either because he used the wrong word or else gave the right word the wrong emphasis or pronunciation he always sounded the outsider that, in fact, he was.

Weir at last took some notice of what had been said. 'A hundred grand's for the punks.' Neither of the other two made the mistake of reminding him that he was inside because he'd failed on a robbery which would have totalled only forty-three thousand pounds.

'I know of a job that'll pay at least a million.'

Weir looked up and his dark brown eyes, almost black in some lights, studied Healey intently.

'Straight, Lofty, this job's worth at least a million.'

Weir lit a cigarette with movements that were strangely effeminate. He had very smooth facial skin, rose colouring, and a small cupid's-bow mouth.

'It's straight, Lofty. A bank which never has less than a million in it. I know how to screw it.'

Farnes said violently: 'You couldn't screw an empty soup kitchen.'

'But my firm did the job.'

'What firm? What job?' demanded Weir.

'I used to work for a firm of architects in Ethington and we did the plans for the bank's strong-room and ...' He was interrupted.

A whistle blew and the warders shouted at the prisoners to leave. Healey hurried to obey their order as he hurried to obey all orders. Weir and Farnes moved at their own pace and the warders did not try to rush them. Weir walked with a slightly mincing gait, and alongside, towering over him, Farnes looked like a huge, awkward bear.

The Angel Hotel in Ethington was an ugly-looking, multi-roofed building from the outside, but inside there was quiet, faded elegance, an air of past prosperity, which held its own charm.

Armitage and Gwen entered the ballroom, decorated in very heavy rococo style, and were audibly assaulted by the noise from two horn-blowing perspiring, red-faced men who were already slightly tight and gaining great amusement from making a nuisance of themselves. Gwen stood up on tiptoe, then said: 'There's Fred—over to the right.' She waved, before leading the way between the tables.

'Well, then, how's everyone? In the mood?' Fred Letts winked. He was always winking. 'Gwen, my love, you're a treat for sore eyes. If you weren't married, I'd get on my knees and propose to you right now, I would.'

'Well, I certainly wouldn't accept you ... Not here,' she added archly. He pulled out a chair for her and she sat down at the circular table. 'Where's your partner, Fred?'

'Dolly wasn't feeling a hundred per cent, so she cried off.' He sat down. 'I got out my little red book and went through all the pages, and know what? There wasn't one of 'em I wanted here, not with you coming.'

'I suppose they were all booked up?'

He chuckled. 'Never mind. Old George is a good sport and he won't mind me having a bit of a shuffle with you. Isn't that right, George?'

'Help yourself, Fred.' Armitage didn't really like Letts, but wasn't certain why. He'd once made the mistake of saying this to Gwen: predictably, she'd told him his dislike was really jealousy that anyone with no background could make such a financial success of life.

'The waiter wanted to know what we'd drink, so I've ordered bubbly,' said Letts. 'Suits you both, doesn't it?'

'How extravagant!' said Gwen.

How unnecessary, thought Armitage, remembering what drinks cost here. At the end of the evening his self-respect would force him to offer to pay their share of the bill and Fred's sense of greed would force him to accept because he could never actually turn down money ... Though if left to pay for everything, he'd be quite happy. Who was it, wondered Armitage, who'd said that of all his possessions, man's self-respect was the most expensive?

There was a roll of drums and the M.F.H., perspiration rolling down his chubby face, stepped out on to the floor. He announced that the hunt supporters' club had raised over two hundred pounds, which would be used to help pay for new kennels for the hounds.

People clapped and cheered and a few made barking noises.

A waiter brought a bottle of champagne to Letts's table, dumped it down, and was about to leave when Letts asked him for a bucket and ice. He muttered that none was available, but finally agreed to have another look when he saw Letts was prepared to get nasty. He brought a bucket filled with ice.

'They're all the same,' said Letts, as he poured out the champagne.

'But at least you don't let them get away with it,' said Gwen. 'George does.'

'Do you?' Letts turned. 'Always the dreamer, eh? I'll tell you. The only thing the average waiter understands is a kick up the backside.' He finished his drink in a few quick gulps. 'What about shaking a leg, then, Gwen? I rather go for a quick-step.'

'For your information, Fred, this is a slow foxtrot—but I don't suppose that'll make much difference.' She stood up.

Letts put his arm round her waist as he threaded a way through the tables to the dance floor. Did he, wondered Armitage, still have hot hands on the dance floor as Gwen had once said he had? A man at the next table smiled and nodded. His bank manager: so charming, he could make the refusal of an overdraft sound as if it were set to music. A couple pushed by, knocking the table hard enough to spill some champagne out of

Gwen's glass, but neither bothered to apologise. He recognised her—a daughter of one of the county's minor aristocracy who was said to have a very good seat in the field. It was certainly of noble proportions.

The band played another foxtrot. It was unusual to hear so many old favourites— presumably, members of the Ethington and District Hunt were not in favour of pop. The next tune had been all the rage when he and Gwen had been engaged. It was interesting to remember that in those seemingly far-off days she'd thought it was really exciting that he was an author and she'd been proud of him.

His thoughts were interrupted. 'Hullo, there, Armitage. All on your own, then?'

He stood up and shook hands with Dudley Broadbent. He knew no one else whose name fitted so exactly. Dudley Broadbent sounded like '12 Taylor's, Romeo and Juliet coronas, Hackermann suits, and sufficient self-satisfaction to arm himself against the sharpest arrows life could fire at him. 'I'm only a temporary widower. Gwen's somewhere out on the floor, in the middle of the pack.'

Broadbent, who'd clearly had quite a lot to drink, decided he might smile. 'You can't sit here on your own. Come on over and have a drink with us ... I don't believe you've met my wife?'

'No, I haven't had that pleasure.' And, as

10

he stood up, Armitage wondered if there was anyone he wanted less to meet than Broadbent's wife. She would be plump, with carefully set hair and over-manicured face, twin ropes of pearls around her turkey-wattled throat, a bosom of much billowing magnificence, pebbles under her tongue, and a carefully cultivated manner for dealing with tradesmen, hawkers, and indigent authors.

Even a cheerful cynic could be wrong. Patricia Broadbent was almost half her husband's age, conventionally slim and with a bosom that did no more than promise, her auburn hair was filled with highlights and had the look of having just come in from an exhilarating blow on the moors. She wore round her slim neck an exquisite piece of early Victorian diamond and opal jewellery, her voice was light and musical, and her manner was unaffected.

'George Armitage writes,' said Broadbent, as if explaining away certain odd facts. 'You're a great reader, Patricia, you must have read some of ... George's. We know each other well enough for that. And I'm Dudley.'

'How very kind of you, Dudley,' said Armitage, before he could stop himself. Broadbent had noticed nothing.

'Some of George's books, dear.'

'I don't think I have,' she said.

Broadbent, puffing slightly, sat down. He emptied a bottle of champagne into a glass for Armitage and then beckoned to a waiter who hurried over and took the order for a fresh bottle. 'Of course you must have read some,' he corrected sharply. 'They're full of exciting things and sex.'

'I don't know that I accept the separation and in any case there's hardly any sex in my books,' said Armitage.

'No sex? But I've been told that's what sells books.'

'True enough, but when I started writing some in, my publishers said it was unrealistic and I ought to stick to things I know something about.'

Broadbent frowned slightly as he tried to decide whether or not Armitage was being serious. Patricia suffered no such doubts. She laughed, and for the first time Armitage realised that her mouth was very slightly lop-sided.

'Do you write under your own name?' she asked.

'That and two others,' he answered.

'Then you can tell me something I've always wanted to know. Why do authors use different names?'

'Because when each book sells as few copies as mine do, one has to write several a year to make a living and publishers don't like more than one book a year under any one name.'

Broadbent was becoming impatient at being left out of the conversation. 'I thought paperbacks did very well?'

'I've often heard that rumour.'

'I read a paperback the other day ...'

The description of the plot was long and inaccurate. Perhaps, thought Armitage, good memory and lucid exposition were not, after all, the prerequisites to being a successful solicitor.

★   ★   ★

Five hours later, as Armitage was thankfully undoing the collar and neckband of his shirt, Gwen said sharply: 'Who was that you spent most of the evening with?'

'Call-me-Dudley.'

'What are you talking about? Why can't you ever answer a question sensibly?'

He sighed. 'Until tonight he was Broadbent and I was Armitage. Tonight he told me to call him Dudley. A beautiful friendship was cemented.'

'When you talk like that you're not in the least bit funny.'

He rubbed his neck, where the base of the stud had dug into his flesh and there was now an indented, red crescent.

She took off her dress and slipped a covered hanger under the straps. 'Is he very important to you?'

'How on earth do you mean?'

'I wondered why you spent so long with him and couldn't be bothered to return to our table?'

'I was being subjected to a lecture on how to write successfully and couldn't escape until it was all over. In any case, you weren't on your own. Or were Fred's hands getting a little too hot?'

'If they were, you obviously didn't give a damn.'

He spoke quietly. 'Spit it out, pet. What's the real trouble?'

She turned her back to him and crossed to the wardrobe.

'If you were bored, why didn't you come over and let me introduce you?'

She took off her petticoat. 'You saw what she was wearing? Her dress must have come from one of the top couturiers and cost a fortune. How could I turn up in what I was wearing?'

'She wouldn't have worried, if she'd even thought about it.'

'Not much!'

'D'you think she worried how I was dressed?'

She didn't answer and finished undressing, slipped on her nightdress, and began to read.

His trouble was, he thought, indulging in his weakness of a love of paradoxes, he was too successful and yet not successful enough.

14

He made enough money at writing for them to be in a position to meet many of the wealthier and more socially prominent people in the area, yet not enough to allow them to offer much hospitality to those same people. More success and they could have mixed freely, less success and they wouldn't have met them in the first place—relieving Gwen of much jealous frustration. He must, he decided, give up writing his present style of books and either produce another *War and Peace* or a ten-volume study of comparative religions.

CHAPTER TWO

Lower Offley Cottage stood a hundred yards back from the road, in a garden whose untidiness clearly betrayed Armitage's dislike of gardening. From the outside, the cottage was very picturesque. Timber-framed, it had a long sloping roof to the south, covered in tiles that were patched with moss, and over the top half of the north wall were scallop-shaped hanging tiles, variegated blue and red, a squat central chimney-stack, and small leaded windows. When they'd first rented it, one year after their marriage, Gwen had said in tones of wonderment that it was the kind of place she'd always dreamed of living in without ever believing her dreams could come true. But in the intervening years they'd met so many people whose houses were not just two up and two down, whose kitchens were not cramped and poorly equipped, whose furniture was not an odd collection from sales, that now if talking to wealthy friends she often referred to the place as 'our hovel'.

He was not certain, looking back in time, quite why or when she'd become so dissatisfied, so envious of the lives other people apparently lived, so certain that the material things in life were what really counted. Perhaps this had always been her character but she had managed to keep the fact hidden, or perhaps she'd changed, little by little.

Except when he criticised books by other authors, he was reasonably self-honest and ready to admit that he didn't earn very much by the standards of most of their friends. But then that was the traditional fate of authors. And at least their garret had two up and two down. But Gwen wasn't interested in traditional fates and seemed unable to discover a sense of humour. She'd read there were authors who made so much money they had to go and live in Switzerland because of British taxation and she felt aggrieved—and ashamed—that he wasn't one of them. For his part he'd have liked to have made more money for normal reasons, yet, perhaps abnormally, he wasn't really disturbed that he didn't. He wasn't interested in large houses, fleets of cars, expensive hospitality, but he was interested in maintaining his freedom to be able to be rude to anyone he didn't like.

He didn't know why his books didn't sell better. Other authors (much less able) sold foreign rights all round the world. His sold to countries whose advances only looked good in their own currencies. His publishers usually said his books were quite good, and friends—though he placed no faith at all in their honesty in this matter—told him they really enjoyed his work. But the public in every country in which his work was published largely remained indifferent to it.

He was in the spare bedroom which he used as an office, typing with three fingers as he'd never learned how to use more without chaos at the keyboard, when he heard Gwen's call. 'George. The car won't start.'

He leaned back, flexed his fingers, then stood up.

'Come on. I'm in a hurry.'

Opposite him was a bookcase in which were all his published books, both in English and foreign editions. An American film company had once become interested in the end book on the top shelf and his agent had even reached the point of discussing how many tens of thousands of dollars he'd be

17

paid. An old pro, hardened by the years, he'd sat back and waited, but Gwen had translated the dollars into pounds and decided what kind of a house they'd buy, how she'd furnish it, and even where she'd get all her new clothes. Of course, the whole thing had never got beyond that and there hadn't even been ten per cent option money. Gwen had been filled with bitter despair, as if the money had actually been paid to them and then taken away. Perhaps that was when her dissatisfaction had crystallised and hardened, he thought, recognising the possibility for the first time.

'Are you coming or shall I call a taxi?'

He hurried out of the room and down the stairs. She *would* call a taxi and leave him with the bill.

She was standing by the front door in the hall, a grand name for a space so small that neither the door of the sitting-room nor that of the dining-room could be opened whilst more than one person was standing in it. She was wearing the trouser suit which she'd bought in a sale a few months before and altered. He could never understand her passionate longing to buy expensive clothes: she had an instinctive dress sense and managed to look smarter than many of their far richer acquaintances in clothes which had cost only a tithe of those the other women wore.

'I must be at Joan's in a quarter of an hour,' she snapped. 'Why can't the garage do something to make the car more reliable?'

'The foreman told me that if they tried to do very much more to it, it would fall apart at the seams.'

Her lips tightened and the lines of angry discontent deepened. She completely lacked his ability easily to overcome the lesser annoyances of life.

He led the way out of the house and along the weed-infested flagstone path to the wooden garage which leaned slightly caterwise from a gale two years back. Once inside, he sat down behind the wheel of the Hillman and checked. The choke was right out. Gwen would have turned over the engine again and again, refusing to push in the choke to see if that would make a difference simply because the car normally needed choke to start: there was a point at which she became so angry that she stupidly and stubbornly refused to try alternative methods to finish whatever it was she was trying to do. He pushed in the choke, floored the accelerator, and tried the starter. The engine fired after a while.

She said: 'You'll have to take me and fetch me: I'm going to be stranded halfway.'

'I'm in the middle of a tricky...'

'It's funny how your work always suddenly becomes tricky whenever I ask you to do something for me.'

He sighed. 'All right. I can carry on to the public library—I've been meaning to check up on something.'

'But you're surely not thinking of going dressed like that? Without a tie, in a shirt with a frayed collar, and a sweater that's only fit for a dog basket?'

'That's just the way I'm going,' he answered, and suddenly there was a snap in his voice which told her he was no longer interested in her opinions or complaints. He had his limit. Below it, he would humour her, blunting her frequent ill-humour with gentle ironic amusement: above it, he became inflexible and no amount of anger or wheedling on her part would make him alter his mind.

Joan lived in a mock Tudor house of unique ugliness. She was a lot older than she hoped she looked and expert attention tried to keep her. She was very wealthy and liked people to envy her possessions. She did not like Armitage.

After dropping Gwen, he drove back to the main road and then the two miles into town. Ethington was a market town that in the past twenty-five years had suffered an expansion which altered its character completely, stripping it of most of its previous charm. Family stores in the High Street gave way to supermarkets, Victorian houses with large gardens vanished and in their place came many-storeyed office blocks, streets were made one-way in a despairing effort to cope with the vastly increased flow of traffic, a large bleak car-park was built where there had once been two rows of Elizabethan cottages, the parish church with its unique small wooden steeple on the ground by the side—legend said a bishop in the time of Henry the Fourth had stolen too many church funds for the steeple to be put on the tower—lost the green lawns which had surrounded it, and the market was banished to the outskirts where it became a ghost of its former self. Amidst so much that had been modernised and ruined, the public library was unusual in that it had been altered yet improved. The main library was large and spacious, there was a separate children's library, reading and reference rooms, and above a large conference hall.

He went into the main library and had a quick word with the head librarian—she always ordered three copies of each of his books—and then carried on into the reference room where he crossed to the shelves with the encyclopaedias. He had picked out the volume he wanted and turned towards the nearest chair before he realised that the only other occupant of the room was smiling at him. For once, he identified a face in time not to give offence. He went round the table and sat down next to Patricia Broadbent.

'Have you come in to do some research?' she asked.

'That would be rather a grand way of saying I've come to check up on a fact or two.'

'I'm glad you take the bother. So many writers these days don't seem to think it's worth while.'

'Shall I let you into a trade secret? If I'm sufficiently authoritative at the beginning of a book on one fact, and can be seen to be, readers will accept me as authoritative throughout the book on all subjects.'

'But what about those who don't?'

'If they're that intelligent, they won't be reading my books.'

She frowned slightly and her blue eyes stared straight at him with disconcerting directness. 'Why are you always slightly embarrassed by talking about your work?' Then she shook her head. 'I'm sorry, I should never have asked that. Dudley's always telling me that I don't think nearly enough before I speak.'

'I'd always prefer that to someone who thinks far too much before speaking ... I suppose I'm slightly embarrassed because people always seem to think they have to praise my books, even when I know that they can't possibly enjoy them because of the kind of people they are.' He changed the

22

conversation. 'And you? What are you doing here? Laying the groundwork for a magnum opus?'

She smiled, and again he noticed how much charm there was in her slightly lop-sided mouth. 'I couldn't write a book—at school I was always very near the bottom of the class for English.'

'In these days bad English is almost an asset.'

Two middle-aged women, dressed in tweeds and looking very earnest, came into the reference room.

'Oh, dear,' Patricia murmured, 'now we shall have to be quiet.'

'I'll be no more than five minutes. How about having a cup of coffee afterwards?'

She hesitated, then said: 'That would be nice.'

'Good. All I need to find is a street plan of Bombay that will give me the names of a few roads. Put them in and people will think I've actually been there.'

She said: 'I'm beginning to think you're really a bit of a reverse humbug. I'll bet you've actually been to Bombay?'

'Only once, and it was a long time ago.'

*   *   *

Weir fitted a cigarette into a long ivory holder and lit it.

23

'I saw Butch Thomas this morning,' said Farnes. He looked across. ''E's a job what could be lined up quick.'

Weir lowered the cigarette holder. 'If that little bastard had the perfect nick on the Crown Jewels, I wouldn't go near it.'

Farnes rubbed his forefinger across the right cheek, unconsciously tracing out the puckered scar which was a memento of a knife fight. He'd thought it a good idea to work with Butch, but if Lofty said no, that was it. He was far from being the thick-headed, strong-arm man his manner sometimes suggested, yet he knew an unquestioning, unhesitating belief in Lofty that was proof against anything, even the failure of their last job which had landed them in jail. It was a strange, and in many ways unlikely, friendship and there were even times when its essential quality changed so that Farnes would feel a responsibility for looking after Weir.

Weir stood up, crossed the poorly furnished room in the house that stood on the outskirts of Whitehaven, and poured himself out a drink. 'Wally, d'you remember that punk in the nick: the one what talked about a job worth a million? What was his name?'

'I've forgotten.' Farnes's chunky, scarred face expressed contempt. ''E was a creep. In for 'is first stretch—at 'is age!'

'But he talked about this bank job.'

24

'Like I talk about paintings,' replied Farnes, naming something about which he knew absolutely nothing.

'I'm not so sure ...'

Farnes poured himself another drink and returned to his chair. There were just occasionally times when he found Lofty inclined to be a little stupid, too ready to believe.

They heard the front door slam and seconds later a blonde came into the room. 'How are things, then?' she asked. She was in her early twenties and attractive, but in a manner which said she'd learned what life was all about. She showed no surprise when she was ignored. 'I've got the grub so d'you want to eat right off?'

Weir at last spoke to her. 'Yeah.'

She left, hurrying because it was clear Lofty was in a bad mood. He scared her because there were times when an inner force seemed to explode inside him. She'd made the mistake, early on, of making some reference to his small size. She never did so a second time.

Back in the sitting-room, Farnes said: 'D'you mind the music on, Lofty?' When there was no answer he went over to the radio and switched it on to the music programme. He had an uncritical love of classical music.

Weir's thoughts continued to be gloomy. Money was running out fast and he needed a

25

good job. That punk in the nick had talked about a million. A bank could hold that much. The punk had claimed to know some weakness in the construction of the strong-room ... The name flashed into his mind. 'The guy's name was Healey. Go find him.'

'Lofty, don't you reckon 'e was just talking?' When there was no answer, Farnes drained his glass. It hurt his pride to be ordered out to look for such a punk.

CHAPTER THREE

There were certain infallible signs that Gwen was angry and one of these was if, at the beginning of a meal, she banged the plates down on the small refectory table, bought at a sale cheaply because it had been badly damaged by woodworm. She banged the two warmed plates down on the table in front of Armitage and then, without a word, left to return through the hall and the sitting-room to the kitchen.

He sharpened the old-fashioned, bone-handled carving knife on the steel and wondered what the trouble was this time? Lack of more housekeeping money, lack of a fixed dress allowance, lack of all the things other women had?

26

He heard her swear in the hall. When she returned she banged down the battered stainless-steel carving dish. Even before carving the chicken, he could be certain it was either under or overdone. When she was angry her standard of cooking deteriorated dramatically. He often wondered whether this was deliberate and, if so, her real desire was to make his life at least as momentarily unhappy as hers. 'How are things going, darling?' he asked. Experience had taught him that it was much better to try to promote an explosion rather than to damp it down.

Again she said nothing before she left. She brought back roast potatoes and Brussels sprouts and the potatoes were obviously not crisp and the sprouts lay in a pool of water. He sighed. He began to carve and cut off one hind leg: the chicken was underdone. 'Will you have some dark meat as well as white?'

His quiet patience fully exasperated her into speech and as she sat down opposite him she demanded: 'Where were you three days ago?'

The question surprised him since he'd expected to find the cause of the trouble was financial. 'Three days ago? ... As far as I know, I spent all day upstairs, working.'

'No, you didn't.'

He was a skilful carver and the three slices of breast he put on her plate were uniformly thin. 'Wasn't I?'

27

'No. And you know very well you weren't.'

He added the lower half of the leg to her plate and then passed it. When he saw the expression of sullen anger on her face he thought how much older she looked.

'You were at the Vandyke café and you weren't on your own.'

He at last realised the cause of her anger.

'You were with Patricia Broadbent. The woman you spent all evening of the Hunt Ball with.'

Deciding it was useless to try yet again to explain about the first meeting, he said: 'I'd clean forgotten I met her in the library.' He spoke lightly 'We had a quick cup of coffee together and, as I remember it, if that coffee wasn't made from acorns, it was made from something worse.'

'Why were you having coffee with her?'

'Why not? We happened to meet at the library . . .'

'You'd arranged to meet her there, knowing I wouldn't be around.' She helped herself to a potato and sprouts. She cut a slice of chicken with more force than was necessary. 'It must be a bit of a shock for you to learn I know about the hole-in-the-corner assignation.'

He still managed to speak pleasantly. 'If you stop to think about it, you'll remember that I'd no intention of going anywhere on Tuesday morning. I was working. But you

28

couldn't get the car started and called me down and when the car was going you insisted I drove you to Joan's. So since my being out that morning was purely fortuitous, how in the hell am I supposed to have had an assignation?'

She was uncertain, but still antagonistic. She seemed to be searching for some flaw in his argument.

As he finished carving, being careful to leave half the bird for the next day, he wondered why she was always so jealous? It hardly seemed worth the bother if he was so poor a husband as she often made out.

Gwen at last discovered a way of continuing to vent her ill humour. 'Mrs. Broadbent ought to have more sense.'

'More sense than what?' he asked wearily.

'To have coffee with a married man.'

'I've never before heard that coffee's quite so incriminating. Or d'you think it's the passport to a quick lay?'

'You're so crude,' she said, almost triumphantly because now it was he who was at fault.

What kind of a lay would Patricia make? he wondered.

*   *   *

The house was in a row of mean, but clean, terraced houses which had no gardens at the front and only small dirt yards at the rear. The door was opened by an elderly woman, almost crippled by arthritis, whose clothing was patched yet immaculately clean. She told Weir and Farnes that Healey was in his room, downstairs next to the kitchen.

Healey's surprise at seeing them gave way to fear and he kept fiddling with his glasses as they sat, Weir on the only chair, Farnes on the bed.

Weir fitted a cigarette into the ivory holder and lit it with his gold lighter.

Healey stared from one to the other of them. 'What . . . like what . . .' His voice was thick because his mouth was dry.

'We was in the market in the nick and you said you knew a good mark, worth a million.' Weir suddenly looked up at Healey.

'Yes . . . Yes, that's right. It's the bank in the High Street in Ethington.'

'No bank usually has a million in it in straight notes,' said Weir.

'But this one does and that's why they had the new strong-room built. It's to do with the way they move money around. Instead of each branch drawing from London, now there's a central cash holding bank in each area and all the other local banks draw from that and send to it their used notes for pulping. That way, when money's shifted to or from London there's only one big movement instead of dozens and like you

30

know, Lofty, London's the big danger point for money snatches. A bloke at the bank was telling me they'd get close to three million in notes at times when a lot of money was being used, like holidays and Christmas.'

Three million, thought Weir. The man who stole that sort of money was telling the world that he was the greatest. 'And you know a way into the bank?'

Healey again fiddled with his glasses. 'Yes. I mean ... It's like this, Lofty. When I said in the nick ... I was doing the plans for the new strong-room and I noticed the way the ingoing electrical mains and the outgoing alarm wires ran in a conduit which was only an inch and a half from the bottom of the concrete of the floor. And I got to thinking that if all the wires were cut ...' He tailed off into silence.

Weir was so surprised it was several seconds before he said: 'That ain't the lot?'

'Yes. You see, I ...'

'You went on about a job worth a million and all you know about it is that the alarm wires run through a concrete floor?'

'But if you could immobilise the alarms?'

'What kind of alarms are there? How many? How thick are the walls?'

'I ... I don't know.'

'What's under the floor of the strong-room?'

'Well, nothing. I mean, it's the earth.'

31

'Jesus! The earth!' Weir said to Farnes. 'Wally. Show the silly bastard.'

Farnes got off the bed. Shoulders slightly hunched, he grabbed the neck of Healey's sweater with his left hand and twisted, his knuckles pressing into the throat. He hit Healey three times, in the body so that there would be no obvious damage, down in the gut because that was the most painful for little risk of serious damage. Healey's spectacles fell to the floor and one of the lenses fractured.

Farnes released the sweater and Healey fell back on to the bed where he dragged air down into his lungs with a rasping sound which changed dramatically as he vomited with explosive force.

Weir, smoking quickly to try to keep away the stench, stared down at the crumpled figure on the bed and saw only a vanished fortune.

Healey, frightened stupid, his body afire with pain, began to babble. There were ways of finding the thickness of the walls because the plans would give it. And the specifications would give the names of the firms who'd supplied the strong-room door and frame, the alarm systems...

Weir stared down at the blubbering man and told himself there was no job here. But it was difficult to forget three million pounds.

CHAPTER FOUR

When they returned from the cocktail party
on Sunday both Gwen and Armitage had
drunk enough to be affected: in his case he
felt slightly deflated, as if the party had
stupidly been stopped at half-time, and she
began to be argumentative. By the time
they'd had supper, on trays in front of a good
fire, and gone upstairs to go to bed, she was
accusing him of having deceived her.

'You knew that Patricia woman was going
to be there, didn't you?' she said accusingly.

He hung his suit, eight years old and
possibly looking older, on a hanger and put
this in the wardrobe.

'Didn't you? Admit it.'

'I'd no idea she was to be there,' he
answered irritably.

'And you expect me to believe that? From
you? The man who hates cocktail parties so
much you usually can't get him to one
however hard you try? Yet when I said at first
I'd got a headache and didn't think it was
worth going, you said you were going
whatever happened.'

He took off his shirt. 'After Angela had
rung up especially to make certain we went, I
thought it would be too rude if we both called
off at the last moment.'

33

'You've never before bothered about being rude.' She undressed so quickly she was in bed before him. She lay back and stared up at the ceiling. 'If it's not too embarrassing, what did you talk about all evening?'

'Your "all evening" was roughly ten minutes. For most of that time, Dudley expounded his views on politics in general and creeping socialism in particular.'

'Then why were you and she laughing together.'

'Listening to Dudley, you either have to laugh or weep tears of desperation.'

'Why can't you ever give a straight answer?'

He finished undressing and put on pyjamas. 'And why can't you take life a bit less dramatically? Meeting Patricia was a pleasant surprise, nothing more, and all the time I was with her Dudley was close by. In those circumstances, in the middle of a cocktail party, even Casanova would have had a job to get anywhere. I'm no Casanova, so I didn't even try.'

She seemed to accept this. 'She ought to have had more self-respect than to spend all the time with someone else.'

He shrugged his shoulders.

'She's much younger than he is.'

'That's fairly obvious,' he said, as he climbed into bed. She moved a little, as if to increase the distance between them.

'She's looking around for someone who'll give her you-know-what.'

'No, I don't know what.'

She didn't explain, being surprisingly embarrassed about putting some things into words. 'It's because her husband's so old.' Her voice was slightly muffled because she'd pulled the bedclothes right up and the sheet was half over her mouth.

'He's only around fifty, whatever he sounds like.'

'But he's not very strong at ... you-know-what.'

'How in the hell can you possibly know anything about that side of his life?' But even as he said that he wondered if she could be right: women had an uncanny instinct over such matters. One thing was for sure. If he were fifty and married to Patricia, she wouldn't lack for you-know-what.

'You'd no right to leave me on my own as you did.'

He lay on his back and stared up at the beamed ceiling. 'You weren't on your own for ten seconds. Fred raced over like a starving man.'

'Don't be disgusting.'

'Isn't sauce for the wife, sauce for the husband?'

There was a short but bitter row. When it finished, because he became silent and refused to be upset further no matter how

35

provoking she was, they each read for a while, then switched off the bedside lights without speaking again.

★   ★   ★

From inside his small dressing-room Dudley Broadbent said in measured tones: 'She is a charming woman.'

That was not quite how she'd describe Laura Relton, thought Patricia, as she lay in the right-hand, single bed.

'I suppose you know she's directly connected to the Westcotts of Theston Manor?' A gentle cough. 'I must admit, dear, I would have preferred you to have been a little ... warmer in your manner.'

He'd wished she'd shown more deference, but this was something she found very difficult to do. If she liked a person it mattered not what was the other person's background, if she disliked a person she found it virtually impossible to simulate an emotion.

'She is an important client of the firm's.'

Laura Relton had come over to talk to Dudley—showing sufficient bad manners to ask him for some legal advice, which he'd hurried to give—when George had been with them. George had whispered a story concerning her that had been as scandalous as it had been amusing. Their laughter had annoyed Dudley.

He came out of the changing-room, as always in a dressing-gown, and went to his bed. He took off the dressing-gown, folded it up, and placed it exactly in the centre of his bedside chair. He did everything very precisely. Sometimes she longed for him to do something in a slovenly manner.

'She has very kindly invited us to dinner next week. I have noted down the date.'

She'd feared an invitation had been given and accepted. Why, she wondered, did he show Laura Relton such deference? Women of her nature were only spurred on by it to even greater imperiousness. It wasn't as if he had to keep her business with the firm—his private income was large enough that if he lost every client on the firm's books he'd still be very well off. It was odd how he, born into wealthy security, should show such respect for money and so-called rank while she, born into a home made poor by her father's long illness, should respect neither. Or was she to some extent deceiving herself? Did she only not respect wealth now because she enjoyed it? She'd certainly envied those with money before she'd married Dudley.

He switched off his light, rubbed the lobes of his ears several times as he always did, settled down, and in a very short time began to breathe deeply, then to snore gently. He always fell asleep very quickly. There were times, when she could not get to sleep because of mental restlessness, that she resented this happy knack of his.

She felt more dissatisfied now, without being able to pin down the cause, than she had for a long time. His snoring increased in volume. Did all men snore? Or only corpulent men, in early middle age, who'd drunk too well? She wondered if George snored, then hastily jerked her mind away from such a question.

*   *   *

The architect's office, just off the High Street in Ethington, had a back door that was secured by only a cheap mass-produced mortice lock. Weir, who was an expert with the twirlers, forced the lock in six seconds. He checked for alarms, though not expecting to find any, because he knew of no one who'd gone to prison for taking too many precautions, then called the other two in from the parked car in which they'd been waiting.

Farnes, for so large a man, was amazingly quiet. Healey, obviously scared, was not and even as he passed through the doorway he slipped and raised a clatter. Weir silently cursed, then shut the door and locked it—in case of patrolling constables—and harshly ordered Healey to lead the way.

They went down into the basement, thirty

feet long, twenty wide, with an atmosphere that was dry yet stale, and switched on the strip lighting because down here they were quite safe. There were wooden racks along two of the walls, divided into small, numbered compartments, and many filing cabinets, each with a roughly painted letter on it.

Healey muttered something about there having been a reorganisation and then searched round for, and found, the cabinet containing the index. From this he discovered the number of the wall compartment in which were the copy plans, made five years ago, of the vault and strong-room of the bank. He took the plans and spread them out on a table and explained them to Weir. 'This is the master drawing which shows the whole thing.' He began to trace out with his finger the areas he described. 'This line marks the actual strong-room. Here are the stairs up to street level and this is the general banking area with the manager's office here.'

'What's the thickness of the walls of the strong-room?'

Healey took a small plastic ruler that was on the table and checked the scale, then read off the thickness of the walls. 'They're three feet, all round.'

Even Weir could not hide his surprise and it was several seconds before he said: 'How are they made?'

'It'll be in the detailed specifications.' Healey went over to one of the cabinets and came back with a file. He quickly checked through the papers inside. 'The walls, ceiling, and floor of the strong-room are three foot concrete of high-quality mix—that's a high proportion of cement and no beach over a quarter of an inch in diameter—with double rod reinforcing, set a foot apart, of inch rods in a two-inch grid pattern.'

Weir leaned over the plan and jabbed his finger down on a straight line. 'What's this?'

'The conduit I told you about. The mains electricity comes through it and one lead feeds the alarm systems within the strong-room and the other carries up through the wall to feed the rest of the bank.'

'So unless the main lead is cut there's no way of breaking the strong-room's alarm system?'

'That's right.'

'How near the dividing wall does this conduit run?'

Healey used the ruler to take a measurement off the plan. 'Just on four feet.'

'And then there's three feet of wall?'

'Yes. And on top of that you've got the ordinary brick wall of the cellar next door which is under a shop, as far as I can remember. You'll see that better in one of the more detailed blueprints.' He pulled out a smaller plan which showed only the western end of the cellar, the dividing wall, and a little of the main banking area.

'What's this mean?' Weir pointed to a thick line.

'That's the double bricking which was built in originally, forty years ago, when the building was first converted into a bank.'

'Then the whole bank's got one protection and the strong-room's got a sight more?'

'Yes. But as I said, cut the alarm wires...'

Weir stared down at the plans which he now understood sufficiently well to appreciate that the job was impossible. Double-thickness brickwork, three-foot, reinforced, extra-strong concrete, a strong-room door built to withstand the worst man or nature could do, an alarm system that couldn't be knocked out without digging down through the pavement outside the bank ... There could be fifty million quid down there and it was going to stay right there. He turned and walked away from the table.

'Shall I bring the papers?' asked Farnes.

What for? he wondered savagely, even as Farnes collected them up. His greatest and most dangerous fault was an inability immediately to overcome failure.

★　　★　　★

Weir stopped the car and switched off the lights. They all climbed out, to be chilled

41

almost at once by the keen wind. From somewhere near came the call, seemingly pain-filled, of a vixen. To their left, the glow of Ethington lightened a segment of the otherwise overcast and black sky.

'Where are we?' asked Healey, his voice jerky because he was shivering so hard.

Weir didn't bother to answer, but merely said: 'O.K., Wally.'

Despite the darkness, Farnes accurately whipped the loop of thin manilla cord up and over Healey's head and pulled it tight around the neck. He forced Healey down to a sitting position and rested his right knee in the small of the back to gain an even stronger purchase. For a time, Healey writhed violently and his fingers clawed so desperately at the rope that he tore off a nail, but then he gave one last shudder, voided, and died. The vixen called again, nearer this time.

CHAPTER FIVE

With typical unpredictability, the latter part of March suddenly produced weather with several sunny, balmy days in succession. Optimists spoke of the beginning of spring, pessimists of the certainty of a rotten summer because unseasonal weather always had to be paid for. Daffodils and forsythia bloomed, woods were carpeted in primroses, and the trees showed their first light greens.

Hermione Grant looked across her sitting-room, remarkable because of its brash mixture of the shoddy and the antique. 'How's Dudley?' she asked, in her slightly croaky voice which often made people think she had a cold.

'He's fine, thanks,' answered Patricia.

'And twice as pompous as ever?'

Patricia could not hide her embarrassment at the question—which a woman of different character might have found amusing.

Hermione stared at her, a bitter, enquiring look in her light brown eyes, then she crossed the room and sat down. She opened a heavily chased silver cigarette case. 'Will you have a fag?'

'No, thanks.'

'You're surely not still trying to cut down on your smoking?'

'I am, but without much success.'

'Why?'

Patricia looked up. 'Why what?'

'Why are you trying to cut down?—as it is, you don't smoke enough to get even a doctor worried.' Hermione prided herself on her direct manner. Others found in it little cause for pride.

'Dudley said I ought to try.'

'I can imagine the tones of earnest piety. And I'll bet he was puffing one of his big fat

43

cigars when he said it.'

Patricia smiled briefly.

'He's very good at telling other people what to do.'

Patricia said nothing and after a while, finding she could provoke neither argument nor criticism of the absent Dudley, Hermione relaxed and took out a cigarette from the box. She was a large woman, large in the wrong places. Had she wanted to, she could have made herself far less remarkable by smartening up, but it seemed she was careless what she looked like or what people thought of her. Although she could easily have afforded to, she seldom bothered to wear anything especially tailored to her by someone who knew how to hide a lumpy figure, but instead wore clothes as unsuitable as slacks. She lit the cigarette and drew heavily on it. 'There's no point in dying of boredom, so if you're not going to smoke, what's your poison?'

Automatically, Patricia looked at her watch.

'Listen. Dudley's up in London at some pompous meeting so you can forget the sun being over the yardarm, or whatever that crap is he always booms out.'

Patricia again felt embarrassed, a not uncommon occurrence in this house, perhaps because, as often, there was some justification for the other's malicious comments. She

44

wished she had the forceful personality to stop Hermione's talking as she did—but it would have taken a second Hermione to succeed at that.

Hermione stood up. 'Will you have your usual?'

'Yes, please, but only a small one.'

'My father always told me never to trust the person who asked for only a small drink. Either he's lying or he's got acid on the stomach.' She crossed to the beautifully inlaid cocktail cabinet, opened the right-hand door, and poured out a large Cinzano and an even larger gin for herself. 'What have you been doing since I last saw you—anything interesting?'

'Not really. Just the usual routine.'

'At being at Dudley's every beck and call?'

Once again, Patricia made no answer. Why did Hermione always jeer at her so for trying to do what Dudley liked? And why had she bothered to come here today? Even if they had been at school together—in the days before her father's illness had brought an end to private schooling—they'd next to nothing in common. Yet Hermione, who disliked so many people and made this clear, was always suggesting they meet . . . only to behave as she had today.

Hermione drank. 'D'you remember telling me you'd met a local author—George Armitage?'

45

'Yes,' Patricia answered briefly. She began to fidget with the pleat of her dress.

'I went to a cocktail party the night before last and met him and his wife. I can't begin to do her, but he struck me as being a welcome breath of fresh air—quite unlike the usual stuffy people you meet at such dos. He's a good eye for the absurd. We had a laugh together, especially over that Mills woman who never goes anywhere without that stinking poodle.'

It was unusual for Hermione to take a liking to anyone she'd just met, thought Patricia. Usually, a new acquaintance was good for only savage criticism.

'We talked books and so yesterday I went to the library to get out one of his to see what sort of stuff he wrote. You know, despite the way he talks, he's trying hard not to be a hack writer.'

Patricia's voice inadvertently expressed her surprise. 'Yes, but how ...' She hastily stopped.

Hermione appeared not to guess at the uncomplimentary inference in the unspoken words. 'Before I left the party I asked him and his wife to a meal tomorrow evening: pity about the wife, but she'll get lost. Of course, you're coming.'

'I? No, I don't think I can, thanks, Hermione.' Patricia put her glass down on the small pie-crust table.

'Nonsense. Just because Dudley's away? Lift your skirts up and show a leg. Stop going into purdah every time that husband of yours goes off. You've got to come because someone must have the patience to talk to that stupid bitch of a wife of his.'

★   ★   ★

Weir parked his Mercedes—for him, a car was the ultimate status symbol—off the High Street in Ethington. Farnes at last relaxed: during the long drive down the motorways they should have had at least three accidents, but the other drivers had given way just in time. When he was annoyed or worried Weir became a crash waiting to happen.

'You stay here in the car,' Weir ordered. 'Then no one won't see us together.'

Farnes, who'd been about to open his door, sank back into his seat. He watched Weir leave and walk away, a small bobbing figure who was remarkable without being memorable. Farnes lit a cigarette. He wondered what the hell was eating Lofty, even whilst he really knew the answer. The bank. Three million quid. The kind of mark every villain dreamed of. Yet the plans they'd stolen had shown them this job was impossible—or, at least, impossible in terms of reasonable risk. So why had Lofty come all the way down here to look at an impossible

47

mark? Maybe for once Lofty wasn't thinking as straight as usual? Still, thinking crooked, Lofty was twice the genius that anyone else was. Farnes shrugged his shoulders and his mind moved on to other things.

Weir would have had difficulty in answering Farnes's questions had they been put to him. A man of keen intelligence, he had the ability to face facts and see them exactly as they were, untwisted by how he'd like them to be. Yet, although he acknowledged this job was impossible, he'd driven over three hundred miles just to study the bank and see for himself its situation.

He walked past two estate agents', solicitors' and accountants' offices, and several small shops and turned into the High Street. To his right was a large island on which was a triangular building with shops below and offices above, with the main road on the far side and a small feed road on the near side. He went up the feed road and this brought him back to the High Street by the cinema and a built-up flower-bed in which massed tulips would not be long in showing colour. A hundred yards down on the other side of the road was the bank.

He stood with his back to a butcher's and studied the bank. The building was oldish and vaguely Georgian in style, with mellow red bricks and red/blue tiles and on the left was a furniture store, on the right a car accessory and electrical appliances shop, with above it a flat. Underneath the bank was the strong-room, reinforced to the point where it could almost survive an atomic explosion, containing up to three million pounds.

Three million quid—that were going to stay there under that pleasant Georgian-style building. Even though Healey had been able to tell them nothing about the alarm system, it was necessary to assume that the conduit which ran through the floor of the strong-room carried out direct alarm lines to the nearest police station. So nothing could be done until the conduit was broken open and the incoming mains electricity, and the outgoing alarm wires, were cut. But there was no way of getting at the conduit.

He lit a cigarette. If only the job were possible, it would really make the name of the man who carried it out. He'd become respected—by the people who mattered— even if he were only knee high to a grasshopper and some incorrectly labelled him a queer . . .

He silently cursed because for once he was unrealistic enough to long for the unobtainable.

He walked on, down towards the cross-roads and the traffic lights. When he drew abreast of the bank he once more looked across and now he stared at the building with hatred because it was denying him something for which he so fervently longed.

That was when he first realised that since the next door had a cellar it might be possible to tunnel under the floor of the bank's strong-room and cut through the concrete to the conduit.

He walked on, more quickly now. Soil could be a problem. Local geological records should show what type to expect. What else didn't he know? The actual construction and strength of the strong-room door and whether it could be burned or blown or whether they should break through the concrete wall? The alarm systems and whether all of them would be immobilised by cutting the wires in the conduit? So much, all vital. But information which could surely be ferreted out since the specifications for the strong-room gave the names of subcontractors and suppliers.

Before anything else, they needed money. So they had to do a small job to get some.

CHAPTER SIX

Detective Inspector French stared down at the leg which had on grey flannels and cheap shoes, stained yellow by the clay, and he wondered why the body couldn't have been planted under the other carriage-way-to-be of the motorway when it would have been in C division's territory?

'Is it all right to dig out now?' asked his detective sergeant, Ippolit.

He didn't answer immediately. Ippolit—the name really didn't seem to go with being a detective—was always rushing things, unconvinced there could be any value in ever taking things slowly, soaking up the atmosphere of a situation.

Ippolit spoke again. 'I've got the blokes waiting.'

French turned and stared at the four constables, in overalls and wellingtons, who were reluctantly standing by to begin the odious task of digging out the body. He then looked back at the inspection pit, dug by a worker to check on subsoil at this point, and wondered how the laws of chance had decided that the contractors would need to know the nature of the subsoil at that point, what negligence there must have been for them not to have had the information a long time before, and why the men digging hadn't been just three inches further to the north when the body would have remained hidden for all time, or at least until the motorway was broken up.

Ippolit was looking more and more annoyed and scornful. He was young, thought French with comforting superiority, and one day he might just slow down enough to learn. Had he studied the scene long enough to see the point in the barbed-wire fence where the two posts had been snapped so that it would be relatively easy to climb over and therefore the ground should be examined very thoroughly for footprints?

He gave the order to start work. For a certainty, he thought, Detective Superintendent Connell would come down from county H.Q. He and Connell had joined the force within weeks of each other and for a time their careers had run parallel, but over the last few years the other had climbed up the promotion ladder and he'd stayed put. He knew, to a large degree, why. He was too involved in his job, putting its true object—crime prevention by crime detection—above everything else: the really successful policeman had to remember that his was a job, not a vocation, to know when and how emphasis should be shifted sufficiently to make the facts appear as seniors would prefer them to appear, to be over tactful because promotion never depended exclusively on ability ...

The pathologist, tall, thin, nearly bald, irascible, arrived, dressed in smart green overalls. He changed from shoes into plastic orange wellingtons, spoke briefly to French to learn the salient features, and then went over to the hole to make the final excavation. From time to time he dictated notes to his secretary, a middle-aged woman who accepted bodies and bits of bodies with far more equanimity than many policemen. Photographs were taken to the pathologist's orders, the photographer, a police sergeant, cursing every time a gust of wind shook the camera's tripod.

The body was lifted out on to a large plastic sheet. The pathologist called French across. 'Throttled,' he said, tracing out the puckered indentation round the man's neck.

Poor devil, thought French. Even after twenty-eight years in the force he still knew compassion.

*　　　*　　　*

Hermione Grant, a pathetically shy person, covered up and compensated for that shyness with a manner so forceful that she repeatedly said things others wouldn't, from a sense of discretion, sympathy, or just plain good common sense. She leaned forward against the table and spoke loudly. 'You know the real trouble with your books, don't you?'

Armitage swallowed his mouthful of delicious ham mousse. 'Of course,' he answered, in a manner that blunted her remark, 'they don't sell.'

'If they did,' said Gwen, 'we wouldn't be having to live in our present hovel.' She'd had too many gin and tonics before the meal, not realising the strength with which they'd been

53

mixed. Her face was flushed and she was sweating very slightly. Her dislike of Hermione had been growing from the moment she'd entered the house.

Hermione might not have heard her. She propped her elbows on the oval, inlaid dining-table, beautiful with the warm patina of two centuries of care, and stared at Armitage who sat immediately opposite. 'I'll tell you. The beginning's fine. It makes me want to keep turning the pages to find out what's going to happen and that's rare today, with all the tripe that's published. You build the characters up and they're real and believable. And then, when you've really got the reader, you introduce violence and ruin everything by destroying reality.'

Armitage was about to speak when Gwen forestalled him. Her sense of antagonism had grown and now she saw a way of expressing it in argument. 'Well—what's wrong with that? Isn't there plenty of violence in life?'

Hermione didn't even bother to look at her. 'Did I say there wasn't?'

'Of course you did...'

'Rubbish! What I said was, reality in George's books ends the moment he introduces violence.'

The tone of voice had been so scornful that Gwen was bewildered anyone could address her like that.

Armitage hurried to speak, to try to draw

54

attention away from Gwen. 'You know what you're calling for, Hermione? The reality of fiction.'

'You know what I mean,' she replied tartly, 'but typically you look for the nearest paradox.'

Armitage smiled. 'So much for my streets in Bombay,' he said, speaking to Patricia.

'What on earth do you mean?' demanded Gwen. He didn't answer her.

Patricia felt distressed, and looked it, as if she were somehow responsible for Hermione. Why, she wondered annoyedly, couldn't Hermione for once keep her tongue in check? Surely she could realise George wasn't very successful in financial terms and therefore it was in appalling taste to talk like this?

Hermione picked up a silver dessert-spoon—George the Third, with her family's crest on the handle—and waved it in the air. 'An ironic detachment from life is all right if you're writing satire. But that's not what you're trying to do. You're dealing with life as it is, yet your books don't recognise that a dead body stinks. It's obvious you know nothing about the colour of violence.'

'Is it?' asked Armitage, at first upset despite his flippant attitude, but then intrigued by what she said and especially by her use of the word 'colour' in such a context.

She put the spoon down, helped herself to the last piece of mousse in the bowl, and

55

resumed talking with a mouthful. 'Just tell me. Have you ever seen real violence? ... And I don't mean on the box which turns it merely into a grisly entertainment.'

He thought back. 'I remember a fight at school that had us all...'

'School!' she said contemptuously. 'The author of your books just would have to go back to school to remember a fight. You've never been terrified in adult life? You've never been so wild from fear, blood-lust, revenge, that you've longed to club someone to the ground and kick him unconscious?'

'Of course he hasn't!' cried Gwen.

Hermione half turned to face Gwen, visibly recognising her presence almost for the first time. 'Why d'you say "of course" like that?'

'George would never hit a man when he's down.'

'Shades of Eton and Harrow,' sneered Hermione.

Gwen was shocked. 'But what you're suggesting is barbaric.'

'What else is violence? And it's because George has been insulated from it all his life, and doesn't recognise it as barbaric, that he can't write convincingly about it.'

Armitage tried to support Gwen, who was now staring at Hermione with bewildered fury. 'You're really only putting forward a proposition that's as old as fiction—an author can't write about something he hasn't personally experienced. If that were true, we authors would have a hell of a life! Just think. Every time I wanted to describe an adulterous association, I'd have to rush off and commmit adultery...'

'Not every time—only the first. And you can't tell me that most authors wouldn't welcome that kind of research.' By chance, Armitage had raised one of Hermione's favourite topics of conversation and she forgot the theme of her previous argument. 'Provided only that he's not called on to pay the price, there isn't a man alive who won't rush off and commit adultery if he can find a woman fool enough.'

An observation properly based on personal knowledge? wondered Armitage. It was difficult to imagine any man had ever pursued her and far more likely that her belligerence was based on resentment. She was an intriguing character, intelligent yet carrying arguments through to absurdity. Or perhaps she did this deliberately, as an extension of her perverse eccentricity? She'd set the table with hand-embroidered place mats and crystal glass, lit beautiful candles in very handsome candelabra, and taken great trouble over the flower arrangements, yet she had not bothered to change out of a shapeless and dirty sweater and a pair of slacks which emphasised the unfortunate size of her buttocks.

'Has everyone finished, then?' demanded Hermione suddenly, bringing to an end her views on the iniquities of men. She stood up. 'Shove your plates along up here.'

Anyone else would have treated the Doulton plates, on which stood the small Axton crystal bowls, with more respect.

★   ★   ★

Armitage had expected a row because Gwen couldn't stand being either ignored or criticised by another woman, more especially a woman she loathed. He sympathised with her, even though a little more intelligence and a sense of humour on her part would have avoided much of her bitter embarrassment. But he had imagined the row would not break until they reached home. Instead, it started as they drove out past the large ornamental wrought-iron gates of Broughton House.

She said fiercely: 'If I hadn't been a guest...' She tailed off into silence, as if to suggest that but for being a guest she'd have verbally wiped the floor with Hermione.

He drew out on to the road. Guest or no guest, Gwen could never be a match for the other woman.

'She's utterly ... utterly terrible.'

'She is a bit of a cough-drop,' he agreed, in conciliatory tones 'But I thought you managed very well...'

'It's all your fault.'

He sighed as he changed gear.

'Well—admit it.'

'Gwen, darling, if you...'

'Don't you darling me after subjecting me to such an insulting time just because you wanted a chance to make sheep's eyes at that Patricia woman. You want something, so it doesn't matter what happens to me. You fixed to see her there, knowing her husband wouldn't be around.'

'I'd no idea she was going to be present.'

Gwen said, with bitter sarcasm: 'You must think I'm really simple to try to feed me that sort of an unlikely story.'

'I promise you, I...'

'Don't bother. I'll not believe you.'

He struggled to remain pleasant. 'Hermione just said it would be a simple dinner. I took that to mean we'd be the only guests.'

'Then why were you so eager to go?'

'I wasn't eager in the sense you mean, but she's an intriguing character and...'

'Intriguing? Is that what you call someone who insults me like she did? Or didn't you even notice because you were too busy staring into that woman's lovely brown eyes?'

'They're blue,' he corrected automatically.

'So you noticed that?' she retorted very quickly.

'I could hardly...'

59

'You could hardly! Yet normally you're so dreamy-minded you've no idea. And what was all that about Bombay?'

He tried to work out what she was now talking about. 'Bombay?'

'You said something about the streets of Bombay and then laughed. Trying to set up a dirty week-end?'

'It would have to be potentially very dirty to want to go there.'

He should have forgone the pleasure of a smart answer. She became wilder in her accusations and eventually he lost his calm and they had a really bitter row that lasted the rest of the way home.

It had not, he thought as he parked the car, been a successful evening. And yet he had enjoyed it until almost the end.

★   ★   ★

Burner Aaron was a small man—except when compared to Weir—with a mobile face which made it very difficult to judge his age. He raised his glass in which was beer. 'Here's the skin off your middle elbow, Lofty.' His appearance might be insignificant, but his skill as a safe-breaker was very high.

Weir didn't bother to return the salutation. He left his own drink untouched. 'The job's worth between one and three million.'

Aaron's expression changed, but strangely

he now looked sad. He sucked on his lower lip. 'What's the mark—a bank?'

'Yeah. A central cash-holding bank.'

Aaron rolled himself a thin cigarette, no thicker than he'd have rolled in prison. When he lit it, half an inch vanished in a burst of flame. 'You'll need a strong crew.'

'I'll get it ... D'you know the firm called Yelting what make strong-room doors?'

'They're good. If that's what you've got, you've got trouble.'

'How much trouble?'

'It'll 'ave a time lock what no one's going to force. Outside plates of special steel with reinforced fireproof insulation, more special plates, a cast-iron plate what's as thick as they can make it and 'as been copperplated to lead off 'eat, and right dead centre maybe thick copper plates reinforced with manganese steel.'

'But you could burn through the lot?'

'Maybe I could, and maybe I couldn't, all depending.'

'What would you need?'

'Something like forty cylinders of high-pressure oxygen, eight of acetylene, and twenty-four 'ours' actual burning time.'

Weir hadn't realised how big a task even the supply of equipment would be. 'Blowing would be easier, then?'

'Sure. Only you ain't going to blow a Yelting door.'

'Maybe we'd better think of going through the walls.'

'How thick are they?'

'Three-feet special-mix concrete and double one-inch reinforcing.'

'Then you won't get through them in under three, four days since you can't make much noise.'

'Come away! If I get a real team...'

'Lofty, you talk to someone what knows, but 'e'll give you the same story. It sounds like a job to forget.'

'Forget three million quid?' Weir spoke angrily. He'd persuaded himself the news from Aaron would be far more encouraging.

*　　　*　　　*

Armitage first heard about the finding of the body when he was in the stationer's at the upper end of the High Street.

'A man with his head chopped right off,' said the young assistant. 'Just imagine! They say the face looks real terrifying.'

'You might say it had some cause,' he replied. 'May I have two...'

'But fancy it happening here!'

He sighed. It was obvious he wouldn't get served until he'd heard all the details. 'Where's this body turned up?'

'Out where they're building the new stretch of motorway. They say he was down in the mud with his head tucked under his arm.'

'Following the precedent set by Anne Boleyn.'

The assistant looked at him with perplexity. 'What's that?'

'The wife of Henry the Eighth. She walks around the Tower of London with her head tucked under her arm.'

'She didn't do that on telly.'

'Then maybe I've got it all wrong. D'you think I could have two reams of quarto typing paper—thick, and not that flimsy stuff?'

She finally served him and he returned to his car. As he sat down behind the wheel and reached over to put the key in the dashboard to start the engine, he suddenly remembered Hermione's words of the night before. He didn't know the colour of violence. She'd been right, even though he didn't agree that it was necessary to know it to be able to write about violence with authority. Even his acquaintance with death had always been second-hand. Did violence colour a scene? People claimed, when visiting places of known past horror, to be able to sense the violence there'd been. Did they, or were they merely reacting to what they'd learned? He had no idea what the answer was. But two miles out of town, presumably not very far from the roundabout which marked the end of the existing stretch of motorway, there was said to be a hole in which a murdered man had lain. For the first time in his life he could observe the colour of murder. He started the engine and drove out of town.

A few cars were parked near the roundabout and some thirty onlookers were as close to the bare levelled earth of the new carriageway-to-be as a uniformed policeman would allow them to get. He joined them.

There was little to see. There was a hole, barely discernible but clearly marked by the excavated clods of earth which were carefully piled on a sheet of plastic, and there were three men, in civvies, who were presumably searching the ground, although from a distance they seemed to be moving without any discernible search pattern.

He lit a cigarette, having to turn his head away from the keen wind to do so, and wished he'd put on a thicker sweater. The scene was bleak, mainly as the result of ripping a new road out of a still generally wintry landscape. But bleakness was different from a sinister impression. Hermione said he didn't know the colour of violence. Here was an occasion when no 'colour' was discernible, even to the most receptive imagination.

He waited, wondering what would happen. In the event, virtually nothing did. One of the searchers left in a car and a quarter of an hour after that the remaining two did the same. There remained the hole, the clods of earth, and the uniformed constable on guard who tramped up and down and from time to time beat his arms against his chest.

★   ★   ★

When Armitage arrived back at the cottage and drove the car into the garage he looked at his watch and saw the time was nearly a quarter to three. He swore. Almost two hours late for lunch. Gwen had real cause to be bitchy.

He went into the house and immediately called out: 'Darling, I'm terribly sorry to be so late.'

There was no answer, but he wasn't surprised because sometimes she used silence as a weapon, as a child would. He went into the sitting-room, but that was empty, and soon he found she was out. He sighed. When she came back, life was going to be difficult. Then he checked on the food and found the nearly cold leg of lamb in the larder and he knew that life was going to be very difficult indeed—by sheer misfortune, he'd chosen to be this late on a day when she'd cooked a joint.

He carried the lamb and four soggy roast potatoes on a glass dish into the kitchen and carved himself three slices of meat and took two of the potatoes. There was some mint sauce, made from dried mint, in a cup in the china cupboard, and he spooned some on to

65

the meat.

As he ate, he thought that she'd probably walked up the road the half-mile to Amy Walters—Amy was the kind of miserable woman who loved hearing about other people's troubles and exacerbating them under the guise of giving consolation. How, he wondered, had the relationship between Gwen and himself reached the low stage it had? If only she could have had a little more sympathy ... He smiled bitterly. How many hundreds of thousands of husbands had said that? ... But she'd see his being late as a personal insult, not as the result of artistic temperament searching for background material and becoming careless of time. Yet, had he been successful and made a lot of money, he was certain she would and could have sympathised with, and understood, the undisciplined manner of an artistic mind. Success was the key word.

He checked his thoughts because they were useless. He and Gwen were what they were, not what they might have been. To continue to criticise her for not understanding him was as futile as criticising himself for not writing best-sellers.

He finished eating, took the plate, knife, fork, and glass out to the kitchen and washed them up, then went upstairs to his workroom. He sat down at the typewriter and tried to resume writing, after reading through the last two pages to regain the thread of the story, but his mind refused to click into gear and instead wondered if friends had to make as many concessions to keep their marriages reasonably stable? What would have happened if he hadn't been able mostly to see the humorous side of things? But once again that was profitless conjecture. All that was certain was that things would have been different.

He stared at the typewriter with dislike. Even at this stage, halfway through the book, he knew it would be no better than any of his others. It would sell roughly the same number of copies, gain the same lukewarm reviews, and perhaps be bought by two low-paying foreign publishers.

Yet he put as much thought, as much mental sweat and agony, into his books as any best-selling novelist, so why should he sell so much less? . . . He grinned wryly. Equality. There must be equality in inspiration! Laughing at himself restored a sense of mental balance and soon he was able to resume work.

★   ★   ★

Gwen didn't return until almost eleven-thirty and by then Armitage's sharp imagination had pictured horrifying accidents of various natures. Then he heard a car stop and a door slam and he hurried to the window and pulled back the curtain, but all he saw were the red tail lights of the departing vehicle. He went into the hall, switched on the outside light, and opened the door for her. It wasn't until she'd pushed past him and had gone into the sitting-room, taken off her leather coat and dropped it carefully on to a chair, that he realised she was slightly drunk.

'So you're back?' she said, slurring the words.

That had been going to be his line, he thought.

'It's nice of you to bother to return.' She stood, nearly under the main beam.

'I've been very worried,' he said quietly.

She crossed to one of the chairs and slumped down into it.

'So where have you been?' A touch of anger tightened his voice.

'Why should you bloody care?'

'I've been sitting here wondering if you'd met with some terrible accident.'

'I'll bet—and hoping like hell I had.' She opened her handbag and brought out a pack of cigarettes: as she tried to take out a cigarette, she spilled several on to the floor.

'Where have you been all this time?' he demanded again.

'Listen to him! The man who had a special meal cooked for him, but who just couldn't be bothered to turn up for it.' She might have been addressing a third person. 'Full of questions now, but he couldn't have cared less about me or the meal earlier on. And why? Because he'd got himself something much more interesting.' She suddenly spoke directly to him in tones of fury. 'How could you, in the middle of the day?'

'How could I what?'

'When you didn't come back I telephoned. You see, I'm not as stupid as you'd like to think.' She began to pick up the cigarettes, at times having difficulty in judging distances.

'You telephoned who?'

'Your tart.'

'Tart? For God's sake. Or are you talking about Patricia?'

'We're not discussing Boadicea, are we?'

'And you think I've been with her?'

'I know so. I saw the way you looked at her last night. When you didn't bother to turn up for lunch I rang her house and the daily woman said Mrs. Broadbent had had a telephone call and had to leave suddenly. Rushing to meet you. She's like a bitch on heat.'

He felt sorry for her. Underneath her crude, drunken anger, he could see hurt. Because of her ridiculous jealousy, she really did believe he was having an affair with Patricia. He spoke softly. 'Gwen, I haven't seen Patricia since I was with you, last night. What happened this morning was that when I

69

was in town a girl in the shop told me a murdered man had been found buried where the new motorway is going. I went out there to see the place, because of what Hermione had said last night about my not knowing the colour of violence . . .'

She laughed with wild bitterness. 'No wonder everyone thinks you write lousy fiction.'

His patience came to a sudden end. 'So where the hell have you been, coming back tight this late at night? Boozing gin with that Walters woman, moaning your head off about me?'

'Gin? Knowing you've been sweating away with that tart of yours? I've been drinking champagne.'

Strangely, he didn't believe her. Which, in retrospect, made him look a fool.

When they went to bed they slept in separate rooms.

CHAPTER SEVEN

Gwen came down from upstairs as he put the two boiled eggs on the breakfast table. He saw the lines under her eyes and the way her forehead kept creasing and merely thought she was suffering a hang-over. But when she was seated she kept fidgeting and then she

70

said, 'I'm leaving you.'

He sat down opposite her.

'I . . . I was going to slip away, but decided I must tell you to your face.' She began to break the shell of her egg.

'But . . .' For a moment he could find no words.

'If only . . .' Her voice quickened and sharpened, as she deliberately remembered all the past hurts. 'If only you'd had the decency not to chase after her so blatantly, I . . . I might have been able to stand it. But to clear off like you did yesterday and just not bother to say . . .'

'I've told you what happened.'

'Lies,' she said violently.

How could two people speak the same language and yet so completely fail to understand each other? he wondered despairingly. 'All right, then. Get on to Patricia and ask her where she went at lunchtime.'

'D'you think I'd lower myself to ask her anything?'

'For Christ's sake, stop being so stupid. I went to the new motorway to see the site of a murder. Where Patricia was, I've no idea.'

She pushed the egg away from her, making no further attempt to eat it.

He stood up. 'I'll get on to Patricia and . . .'

'It doesn't matter what lies you've arranged between you. I'm leaving you.'

'It won't be lies . . .'

'Why can't you at least have the courage to admit the truth?'

As she looked at him, he understood that there could be no proof strong enough to convince her he was telling the truth. She was determined to believe he had committed adultery. He slumped back in the chair and wondered if other couples reached the end of their marriage road in so pedestrian a manner: casually, over the breakfast table, as if discussing the weather?

She spooned sugar into her coffee, stirred it, and then didn't drink it. She looked at her wristwatch.

'Where the hell d'you think you're going to stay?' he asked. 'What are you going to do for money?'

'I'm going away with someone.'

He knew immediate disbelief. 'You don't mean with a man?'

She nodded.

'Who?' His voice was thick.

'Fred.'

'Fred Letts? You're going away with him? That creep?'

'Just because you don't like him.'

'Am I supposed to like the man my wife says she's running away with?' His voice rose. 'If that little prick sets foot inside this house, I'll smash him.'

'He won't.' She suddenly stood up, moved

back the chair, and left. He heard her go up the stairs and across to their bedroom, immediately overhead. He stared at his egg. What did twentieth-century, civilised man do when his wife said she was going off with another man? Have a punch-up? Argue? How could you have a reasoned argument over who was to have your wife? Convince her he'd been telling the truth? But all she wanted was justification for the course of action she was determined to take, so there could be no convincing her. In any case, was she worth the trouble?

He heard a car approach and stop. She crossed the bedroom and descended the stairs. A car horn sounded twice. He went to the door of the dining-room and opened it as she stepped down into the hall, handbag in one hand, white suitcase—which he remembered he'd bought for her honeymoon—in the other.

'You fixed up all this last night, before you came back here,' he said.

She put the suitcase down and opened the front door.

'Yet you hadn't the guts to say a word until just now?'

She walked out. Fred Letts was behind the wheel of his Rolls-Royce and he was staring at the house. When he saw Gwen he leaned across and opened the passenger door, but did not leave the car. She got in and for a brief moment there was confusion because of the suitcase, then Letts lifted it over on to the back seat. The Rolls moved away, quietly, silently, luxuriously.

Armitage cursed, as violently as he knew how.

★   ★   ★

Armitage stared through the sitting-room window whose curtains were not drawn, even though it was long since dark, and he dully wondered how Gwen was getting on?

Fred Letts. How in the name of hell could she have gone off with him? Fred was a clown, the perpetual juvenile with hot hands, always trying to drop things down the front of dresses, watching every mini-skirted woman who looked as if she might bend over because he'd once been told that some did not wear pants.

He reached over for the gin and tonic and drank it quickly, aware that he was already slightly tight. He'd often rowed with Gwen, but this was part and parcel of life and marriage. He'd never had an affair with another woman, although there had been clear opportunities. Yet she'd been ready to believe he'd been having an affair, even though she'd no proof whatsoever. Or was this the excuse she'd been searching for, to cover her own affair that had been going on

74

for weeks, months?

What was she doing now? He looked down at his watch and initially had difficulty in making his eyes focus. It was just after eleven o'clock. Probably they were in bed together. Sometimes she displayed the kind of uninhibited lust that made a man crazy . . .

He finished his drink and poured out another, as he cursed his vivid imagination.

★   ★   ★

The wages snatch from the supermarket, carried out to supply cash for running expenses, was as meticulously planned as were all Weir's jobs.

Farnes and Kirk, hired for this one operation, burst into the manager's office as the day's takings were being counted out and placed in night-safe bags. The manager and his assistant were brave but stupid: they tried to fight, even though the money wasn't theirs and was covered by insurance. Farnes and Kirk used their coshes with vicious skill and when they left both the manager and his assistant were unconscious and seriously injured. Days later, a specialist was going to have to tell the manager's wife that it was possible, perhaps probable, he'd suffered permanent brain damage and there might be little chance he'd ever be able to work again.

★ ★ ★

Detective Inspector French was conscientious to the point where there were times when he despaired of ever being able to do his job properly. With the division short of manpower, work initially became a question of priorities—which crimes were serious enough to be properly investigated?—and he'd never felt himself capable of deciding priorities because, unlike many, he did not see any crime as capable of being measured solely by the value of the goods stolen or the injuries inflicted: he could enter the grief of an old woman swindled out of her laboriously saved few pounds, a crime not serious enough to rate a separate statistical mention.

One of the two telephones on his desk rang. Dabs at county H.Q. identified the murdered man from the motorway as Brian Healey, aged forty-seven, married but separated, not long out of prison. How had he, no true criminal, become mixed up in something vicious enough to end in his being murdered? French sighed. This case was going to be a real bitch.

★ ★ ★

'Forty cylinders of oxygen and eight of acetylene?' The old man scratched his bald head. 'That's a whole lot of gas.'

76

'How much would it weigh?' asked Weir.

The old man scratched his head again, reached into his pocket and found a stub of a pencil, picked up a scrap of paper from amongst the confusion on the mantelpiece. Very laboriously, occasionally speaking aloud, he worked out the figures. 'Forty at one and an 'alf hundredweight ... 'Alf again ... Sixty ... And another eight makes ... No, it don't. Twelve ... Just over three and a 'alf ton, Lofty.'

Weir hadn't been expecting so high a figure. 'So how much would it cost?' he asked, in a disgruntled voice.

'A thousand quid.'

'You've got to be joking!'

The old man didn't bother to answer. He was too old to joke any more.

★   ★   ★

Weir stared at the electric fire. There was a bank. At all times it had in its strong-room at least a million in notes. There was an alarm system, some—or all—of the wires of which ran through the floor, very close to the bottom surface. It had three foot reinforced concrete walls, that could not be blown or cut through in the time available. It had a door which could not be blown, but might be burned if sufficient oxygen could be provided, but the bottles of gas weighed over

77

three and a half tons and where could the carrying vehicle be hidden during the unloading?

He finished his whisky. Why go on belting his head against a brick—concrete—wall? But even as he decided that the job *was* impossible, another part of his mind said that the more impossible it was, the greater the reputation of the man who did it.

CHAPTER EIGHT

April began by living up to tradition, being totally unpredictable weather-wise, with days starting fine and warm and ending with heavy showers, or vice versa. Hermione Grant's gardener was a morose individual who seemed to scorn the vagaries of weather and who often muttered darkly to himself. He had reason to. She was constantly wanting the garden altered, never content to let any part rest and establish. He continued to work for her only because she paid him a very good wage and because he was a character who needed some major grievance in life against which he could rail. It had just stopped raining and she was having a row with him when Patricia entered the drive in her red Morris 1300. Hermione stamped over to the car. 'Come on in and have a drink. The bloody man's planted the wrong bulbs yet again.' Her powerful voice carried to the gardener: he shrugged his shoulders and returned to work in a state of pleasurable gloom.

'I can't really stop,' said Patricia, through the opened window. 'I've just come for some money.'

'For one of your collections? Well, you won't get anything out of me unless you come in for a bit.'

Reluctantly, yet conscious of the fact that Hermione could be very generous, Patricia climbed out of the car and followed Hermione into the house.

Hermione poured out a sherry for Patricia and handed it to her. 'I suppose you know about George and Gwen?' she asked, abruptly.

Patricia shook her head and looked worried. 'No. I haven't heard of either of them for days. What's happened? Nothing terrible, I hope?'

'She's left him and gone off with Fred Letts.'

'Gwen's left him? What on earth's caused that?'

Hermione sat down, a gin and tonic in her hand. 'Surely you can guess?'

'Why should I be able to?'

'I just thought you might.'

Patricia spoke in what, for her, was a sharp

79

voice. 'Are you suggesting something?'

'Suggesting something? For God's sake, Pat. Can't I speak without your jumping down my throat?' Strangely, there were times when Hermione's directness deserted her and she'd never speak her thoughts. 'Have you ever met Fred Letts?'

'No, I don't think I have.'

'How any woman could go anywhere with him! Still, he's rich, through no fault of his, and that's what interested Gwen.'

'How terrible for George.' Patricia fiddled with her large solitaire diamond engagement ring. 'Have you spoken to him since it happened?'

'No, I haven't.'

'I wonder how he's taking it?'

'Pretty badly. Underneath he's really terribly soft-hearted. If he weren't, he'd have belted that silly bitch of a wife of his and brought her to heel years ago.'

'We must go and see him, in case there's something we can do to help.'

Hermione drank. 'There's no point in my going,' she said finally. 'He won't be interested in seeing me.'

'What do you mean? He'll be interested in seeing anyone who can take his mind off what's happened for a bit. You're not scared, are you?'

For once, Hermione looked uncertain of herself.

Farnes arrived at five in the afternoon, just after a heavy shower had given way to sunshine. Water dripped from his raincoat as he went through to the kitchen. 'Lofty,' he said excitedly, 'I've found a bloke what's for us.'

'Great,' said Weir, through a mouthful of bread and butter. 'You've done great.'

Farnes was clearly pleased by the praise, as scant and as patronising as it had been. He took off his mackintosh and threw it over the back of one of the wooden chairs and then took the lid off the teapot to see if there was enough tea for him. ''E's a bloke called 'Arry Jenson and 'e works for the Buckland Security firm.'

'How d'you get on to him?'

''E visits one of the local Toms, regular.'

'Is he married?'

'Yeah, with two kids. I 'ad a shufty round where 'e lives and saw 'is missus. Looks a nice lay: funny she don't give 'im all 'e wants.'

Weir shrugged his shoulders. 'So what about the Tom?'

'She'll play for an 'undred. Tried for more, of course, on account of us doing 'er out of a regular, but I persuaded 'er.'

Weir could imagine the vicious threats

81

which had been used.

★　　★　　★

Armitage very soon appreciated there was a
limit to the self-pity he could allow himself.
Life went on and he had to go with it. He
resumed work and was surprised to discover
that the writing was no more difficult than it
had been before. Cooking was a
time-consuming business, but he began to
think himself not at all bad at it and to try
more advanced dishes. Even mental pictures
of Gwen's making love to Fred began to take
on a certain dream-like quality so that their
capacity to hurt was very much lessened.

He was helped in reconciling himself to
what had happened by both Patricia and
Hermione. Patricia called occasionally, always
during the day and for a short time, though
her visits tended to lengthen; Hermione came
more frequently and often stayed until late at
night, clearly finding as much pleasure in the
visits as he did. They had fierce arguments,
over nothing of the slightest importance, and
discussed anything and everything except
marriage, an exception which suited them
both.

It was Hermione who told him about the
flat. 'You know you've been talking about
clearing out of this place?' she asked, as she
settled back into, and overflowed, one of the

armchairs.

He nodded. 'The present lease runs out very soon and although I like the area out here, I'm sure I'll be happier somewhere different.'

'Have you thought about living in town for a while? There's a pleasant little flat in the High Street in Ethington that's going to be free very soon. Friends of friends have been living there, but the husband's being moved up north somewhere.'

He far preferred the countryside, but living in the town would be one more way to cut himself off from his previous life. 'It sounds all right, but what's the level of rent? Some places in Ethington these days are up in the millionaire class.'

'It won't be one of those because Ramsey certainly couldn't afford it. I'll see if I can find out for you. Oh! ... By the way, it's on top of a shop, but I don't suppose that'll worry you?'

He smiled. 'My pride lessens as the rent drops.'

★   ★   ★

The photographs were taken when Harry Jenson and Pam were on her bed, both naked, and he was aware of nothing but his lust-filled body and the fact that she was not refusing even his most outlandish requests.

83

Incredibly, he first thought it was some kind of perverse joke. Then the two men, brutally self-confident, coarsely amused by what he'd been doing, gave him the facts very simply. The photographs could be sent to his wife, with copies distributed round his home town, or he could find out full details of the security equipment installed by his firm in three banks. He discovered he was a coward and agreed to co-operate.

He was a man with a conscience and after he'd carried out their orders he hated himself for what he'd done. He worried so much that on Friday, a wet and windy night, with the roads in a treacherous state, he drove into an S-bend thirty m.p.h. too fast. The car skidded and hit a telegraph pole.

A post-mortem showed no alcohol in the blood and no heart attack, an inspection of the car showed no discernible mechanical fault, and the police report stated that the real cause of the accident was impossible to ascertain beyond the obvious fact of too great a speed.

★   ★   ★

Weir looked down at the detailed plan of the bank and its defences he had drawn out on a very large sheet of white cardboard. He stood up and eased his back and briefly stared out of the window as he told himself it was time he finally admitted the bank job *was* impossible.

He'd coloured the alarm systems in red. There seemed to be red lines everywhere. The outer windows and doors were connected up to contact alarms, the walls to sensor alarms, the strong-room had a separate and far more sophisticated system. Within the strong-room was a master unit with time clock. There were contact and heat sensors in and around the door and vibrational sensors in the walls and ceiling. There was a vacuum alarm: ten minutes after the strong-room door was shut for the night a small air pump drew off air into a container until there was a discernible drop in pressure and then any subsequent rise in pressure triggered an alarm. And finally, as if these defences weren't enough there was the closed circuit TV camera focused on the door, transmitting to a receiver at street level which was normally covered with a shutter like a night safe. A patrolling constable had only to find the screen dead or, more dramatic, someone in the act of attacking the door, to sound the alarm.

Weir left the table and poured himself out a really strong whisky. He felt a bitter, grudging admiration for the firm of Buckland Security. They could never have imagined circumstances would so jell together that anyone would learn there was a chance of cutting off all electricity to the vault and so immobilise the alarms, yet they'd clearly accepted the possibility because they'd installed the TV camera. So now it didn't do a goddamn bit of good to know it might be possible to break through the floor and cut the wire in the conduit ... Either the TV watched the break-in or the TV screen was blank—in either case, the alarm would go out.

He threw his empty glass against the wall.

CHAPTER NINE

The rent of the flat, on two floors above a car accessories and electrical appliances shop, was low because it had never been modernised and was in need of considerable decoration. Armitage was unworried by such matters. Unless there was particular reason to do so, he seldom noticed much about the ordinary things around him, and in any case the flat had a restful, pleasant atmosphere which turned it into a home immediately.

When Patricia first visited him there, she carefully explained that she had just called to see how he was settling in and if there was anything she could do to help. The next time, several days later, she did not bother to give a reason for her calling and she stayed so long that she was late for a hairdressing appointment. On her third visit he tried to lift their friendship on to a more intimate level, but failed, though in a way that left him hope for the future.

Hermione became a frequent visitor, often bringing the food for dinner. With no reputation to lose, in the sense that no one could believe any man would find her remotely sexually attractive, she was careless about how long she stayed and how late the time when she left.

He'd delivered his first manuscript since Gwen had left him to his publishers and he received the usual letter of acceptance, neither praising the script nor criticising it. He had lunch with his editor—an eagle-eyed, middle-aged woman of indeterminate sex—and didn't really enjoy it because she told him that a writer he knew well was now selling over ten thousand copies in hardbacks. His agent, who could have been dead for months, wrote to report three foreign sales, one of which, to France, was of some financial consequence.

He heard from a woman who'd always disliked him that Gwen and Fred were in Mallorca, staying in the White Suite at the Formentor Hotel. When he showed indifference to the news, the woman disliked him even more.

Weir drove his Mercedes down the M1 to Newport Pagnell and the service area and parked in one of the lines of cars behind the restaurant and shops. After only ten minutes, Lou Dunder joined him in the car. Dunder was a broad, cheerful man, with a very noticeable squint. 'How's life, then, Lofty?' he asked.

For a short while they exchanged news, then Weir said: 'I've got a job, Lou, a big one. Only it means burning through a door what's watched by telly with the law looking in on a screen whenever it wants to during the night. It ain't no good smashing the camera, because if the law sees a dead screen up top it's the alarms. So how do we get at the door?' His voice expressed a little of his angry bafflement.

Dunder lit a cigarette and, after the first draw, fiddled with it. 'What's the camera doing? Is it panning backwards and forwards? Seems to me, Lofty, if it was still then maybe there'd be time to use a second camera to take a shot on tape of the door, splice the tape up to give continuous running, and show the pictures on the screen so the law don't see nothing different.'

It was so simple a solution that Weir wondered how he'd ever missed it. Dunder must think him soft in the head.

★   ★   ★

Although Ethington High Street had changed so much in character over the past years, there were still a number of flats above the shops and offices. Weir hired a front man to go round the local estate agents to try to find a flat immediately and this man succeeded because the owners of one building were trying to get a higher rent than was reasonable. Weir put two men in the flat to keep watch. Tony Ricard, of direct Italian descent and very Italian in looks, and Bert Smith, as English as fish and chips in vinegary paper, who'd once been a professional boxer of small skill but great strength. They got on well together and during all the time they kept watch there was not one serious argument between them.

Over many days and nights of observation they discovered several important facts. The High Street lay within two beats, one covering the north side and the other the south, and because of the concentration of valuable property patrolling constables from each beat were frequently up and down it. On the face of things, so much unchartable activity made any operation at street level highly dangerous. But between 9.45 and 10.05 at night the roads seemed always to be empty of policemen. For a time, Ricard and

Smith puzzled over the fact, but then Ricard realised the reason. Duty hours for uniformed policemen ran from two in the afternoon until ten at night and from ten at night until six in the morning. Human nature being what it was, the men on late turn were eager for prompt relief and therefore made certain that at the right time they were as near to their police station as their beats allowed them to be—a position known to their reliefs—and not necessarily where regulations said they should be. So for about twenty minutes it should be reasonably safe to check the TV screen.

On the last Friday in April, a warm evening with a light breeze, Ricard, wearing a P.C.'s uniform, walked up the High Street at five to ten. He stopped by the bank, turned his back on the two men and one woman who waited at the bus-stop for the last bus of the night, and lifted the flap over the TV screen. He saw a section of wall in which was a massive door, convex in shape, with a central spoke wheel. The camera was fixed. He replaced the cover and walked on, round the corner where a car waited for him.

The bank job was on.

*　　*　　*

Patricia, dressed in a light summer frock over which she'd put on a sweater because out of the sun and indoors there was an edge to the day, sat back on the settee. She fidgeted with the straps of her handbag, then said: 'Dudley's going over to Amsterdam for a week-end on a lawyers' conference. It sounds rather boring to me, but he seems to be looking forward to it.'

She'd tried to speak lightly, as if she were just making conversation, but Armitage knew that what she was really telling him was that they'd be able to meet for longer than usual. Although she was a person who hated subterfuge, she could not bring herself to say outright what she meant. Her loyalty to her husband remained strong, paradoxically even whilst it was being undermined by her emotions. He remembered her last visit, when their passions had suddenly risen until it was only at the last moment she had drawn back from what had seemed inevitable. Perhaps, he thought, he should feel guilty at the pressure he was putting on her, but his emotions were as involved as were hers.

'Don't look like that,' she said suddenly.

'Don't look like what?'

'As if ... You looked almost cruel, George.'

'Wind,' he said, turning into a joke something very far from a joke. 'If Dudley's off on the rampage, you can come and have dinner with me, can't you?'

'Dinner? I don't think...'

'You can't refuse, because it's my birthday on Saturday and I always go mad and buy a bottle of champagne and I can't possibly drink it on my own.'

'I'll bet you really can.'

'Not without a lot more wind.' He grinned. 'Anyway, too much champagne makes me very mournful and I sing all the songs I used to sing when I was young, healthy, and optimistic. I have a terrible voice.'

'You're talking like an old man of ninety...' She again fiddled with her handbag. 'I don't think dinner ... Unless you mean...'

'I don't mean at a restaurant, Pat.'

'Then I don't think I should come.'

'Why not?'

'You know as well as I do. I ... I just can't trust myself. George, if you really want to have dinner here, ask someone else as well.'

'That would be like using a twizzle stick on the champagne.'

She smiled briefly. 'I still think you should.'

'Very well. I'll ask the Grumonds,' he said, naming a middle-aged couple they both knew who were totally boring in character.

She looked at him almost hopelessly. 'You're impossible.'

'Quite impossible. My form master prophesied I would come to a very sticky end. Then it's all fixed up for Saturday and there'll be you and me and just your shadow as chaperon.'

She still hesitated. 'Only on one condition.'

'Which is?'

'That you promise not to . . .' She stopped.

'Not to make love to you? All right. Scout's honour.'

Neither of them believed what he said. He stood up and crossed to the small side table on which was a bottle and two glasses. 'Can I insult your palate with a glass of Cyprus sherry?'

She nodded and watched him pour out two glassfuls. 'I suppose you know that I'll now spend the rest of this week staring my conscience in the face?'

He spoke softly. 'Then don't. Send it away on a long holiday. You make the world too severe a place, Pat, where the only thing you're prepared to enjoy is a hair-shirt.'

'Stop using words to twist everything. You must know how I feel, or if you don't, you're not a very nice person.'

He handed her one of the glasses, bent down, and lightly kissed her cheek. 'I know that you've got more loyalty in your little finger than most people have in their whole body. You're a living anachronism.'

'I hate it when you become cynical.'

'How else can I save myself from despair?'

He went over to the other armchair, sat down, and lifted his glass. 'Here's to us.'

She raised her glass, but said nothing.

Some twenty minutes later, after having done all she could to keep the tenor of the conversation light, she stood up and smoothed down her frock. 'I must leave. I told Hermione I'd be with her for lunch at one o'clock sharp and that cook of hers gets terribly upset if anyone's late.'

He wondered if she always said to Dudley that she was visiting Hermione throughout the time she was away, or whether she ever admitted where she was actually going or had been? He doubted that. Dudley was clearly a man who 'owned' things and would be infuriated if he thought someone was trying to deprive him of one of his 'possessions'.

'Get here as early as you can on Saturday,' he said.

She nodded. 'Don't forget your promise.'

He crossed forefinger and middle finger of each hand and held them up for her to see.

They went out into the passage and down the steep back stairs to the back outside door. Beyond was an area, part loading bay for the shop, part garden, surrounded by a tall brick wall in which were two large wooden doors to allow vehicles in and out and one small wooden door for pedestrians. He knew how much she hated using this back exit because of its connotations of secrecy and duplicity, yet equally she did not want to use the front door where the chances of her being seen by someone she knew were so much greater. They said a hurried and apparently unemotional goodbye, then he opened the small door and she stepped out and left. He heard her shoes, clacking lightly on the pavement, as she walked considerably quicker than she normally did.

He returned, past one of the two raised flower-beds in which he'd planted some Sweet Williams: they looked floppy and it was odds on they'd not survive. He still hadn't got green fingers.

If only there were a quick and painless air crash on the way to Amsterdam. ... He grinned, as he went back inside. The other passengers in the plane would find that a somewhat selfish attitude!

$$\star \qquad \star \qquad \star$$

Saturday was fine and warm and in the large orchards to the north of Ethington the pear trees were covered with blossom while the apple trees were about to break. Bluebells carpeted woods that were relatively undisturbed and thorn hedges were in leaf, with thorns still soft, not yet having developed rapier-like points.

By circling round and coming into the town from the east, Patricia was able to avoid the holiday traffic, now clogging the roads as it returned from the coast. She reached the

High Street up at the northern end and parked at the back of the Gwelf Supermarket, open late. She went inside and bought half a pound of pressed beef, then a jar of baby beets. Dudley, who was used to the luxuries of life, had a strange liking for the plebeian pressed beef—he said it reminded him of his schooldays which, he claimed, had been very happy. As she waited in the queue to pay, she wondered why she was buying the food now when there would have been time to get it on Monday? She knew the answer, yet refused to acknowledge that she did: by worrying about feeding her husband on his return, she was reassuring herself that her loyalty to him was still paramount, even when on the way to spend the evening with another man.

She left and returned to her car and put the package on the front passenger seat. She drove out, along Taverne Road, past a memorial to some otherwise forgotten Victorian inhabitant of the town, and went into the small council car park she used whenever visiting Armitage. It had an honour ticket barrier and she bought a ticket, though few others would have bothered at this time on a Saturday night when the chances of the car's being checked were virtually nil, put the ticket on the car's dashboard and left after locking up.

She crossed the road and went along to the small door in the brick wall, opened it, and went in. She hated this furtive entry as much as she hated her furtive exits.

The door into the flat was open and on the way in she rang the bell twice. Armitage appeared at the head of the stairs and the warm smile of welcome on his face temporarily banished all her worries. When she reached the landing he kissed her. She quickly moved away, opened her handbag and took out of it a small packet in white tissue paper. 'Happy ninetieth birthday, George!'

He undid the paper to find inside a box in which was a corkscrew, of the kind where turning the handle first drove the corkscrew into the cork and then pulled it out. The last time he'd seen her, he'd casually said his only corkscrew was worse than useless since it was breaking corks rather than pulling them. 'This is exactly what I wanted and as a matter of fact I was going out tomorrow to buy myself one.'

She smiled. 'That's very clever of you since tomorrow's Sunday and all the shops will be shut.'

'Must you be quite so literal?'

'I'm just drawing your attention to your sublime indifference to the facts.'

'Didn't you know I was a writer?'

'Who's only been to Bombay once?'

They went into the sitting-room, both responding to the atmosphere of sparkling fun which had sprung up immediately and which had effectively banished, or at least silenced, any uncertainties she had had.

'And now to the great moment,' he said. 'I'll tell you, I've worn blisters on my tongue, waiting to open up the champagne.'

He went into the kitchen and took out of the fridge the bottle of Moët et Chandon, which began to frost almost at once. Back in the sitting-room, he pulled off the foil, unscrewed the wire, and eased out the cork with his thumbs.

He poured out champagne and passed her one of the flute-shaped glasses. 'Cheers.'

'Happy birthday once more. You know, George, you haven't said which one it is yet? If it's not your ninetieth, is it your thirtieth?'

'Now there's a delicious sense of tact! I'm thirty-eight and all too often feeling every one of them.' He drank. 'By the way, I've been a very lazy cook and settled for two duck in orange sauce from the deep freeze place. Have you ever tried them?—I think they're good.'

She shook her head. 'Someone told me that place has a lot of nice things, but Dudley refuses to eat anything that's been deep frozen. Years ago, he read somewhere that freezing destroys all taste and can even be dangerous and now nobody can persuade him differently.'

'I'll bet if you served him a portion of this

duck he'd eat it with gusto and never guess.'

'On the contrary, he'd know at once. I'm such a poor cook that if it's all that good he'd be absolutely certain it couldn't be my cooking.'

It was odd, he thought, how often Dudley appeared in their conversation. Almost as if they deliberately kept reminding themselves that he existed.

★   ★   ★

Ricard, who was driving the stolen Jaguar, braked to a halt in front of the electrical appliances and motor accessories shop. Farnes and Smith climbed out. They wore caps, dark trousers, and sweaters, blue plimsolls, and close-fitting gloves, all recently bought from multiple stores. The caps were worn so that much of their foreheads was concealed, a very simple method of disguise that was remarkably effective in confusing the ordinary, untrained observer.

The door to the flat was locked. Farnes, taught by Weir, opened it with a slide of plastic. He and Smith went inside, shut the door, took off their caps which they folded and put in their pockets, and pulled nylons over their heads.

Farnes was the larger man, yet he made even less noise than Smith as they climbed the stairs. They heard the hum of conversation from the front room. Farnes waited outside, cosh in hand, whilst Smith searched the rest of the flat. When Smith returned and reported, with a shake of the head, Farnes took hold of the handle of the door with his left hand, turned it very slowly until at full tension, then flung open the door.

CHAPTER TEN

Patricia was talking about her last visit to the theatre in London when the door of the sitting-room slammed open and two hooded men came in, coshes in their hands. She and Armitage stared at the men with, unknown to them, similar expressions of complete disbelief: the episode was so unexpected, so contrary to their normal world, they refused initially to accept the evidence of their senses.

Farnes said: 'Belt up and don't do nothing and there won't be no trouble.'

The words forced them to acknowledge that this was reality. Armitage looked across at the window and began to rise from the chair. Farnes reached him in two strides and hit him across the side of his head, caterwise behind the ear, and his head was blasted with a searing white light and he collapsed back on to the chair.

As the world collected itself together,

Armitage suffered a stabbing pain which raced round his head from the point where he'd been hit. He saw Patricia staring at him, her face twisted with terror and shock, and his only thought was the desperate need to raise an alarm. Perhaps he could hold off the man long enough to smash a window and shout for help? He went to throw himself over the side of the chair, intending to roll across the floor, but the man seemed to read his thoughts because the cosh came down a second time, with more force, and blasted him into unconsciousness.

Patricia opened her mouth to scream. A duster was jammed into her mouth and her scream became no more than a gurgle. Her hands were grabbed and viciously pulled behind her back, twisting her round in the chair and partially over the arms, and they were secured together with sticking plaster. The man came round the chair, took hold of her legs at the ankles and jerked them up in the air, spilling her back into the chair. She tried to kick and he reached over and belted her in the stomach and she gasped and thought she was going to vomit. She let him strap her legs together. Incredibly, she still knew sufficient modesty to be worried because, although she was wearing tights, her legs and thighs were exposed. He dropped her legs and she slithered off the chair, thumping her hip on something.

Armitage began to recover consciousness. A voice, seemingly from far away, told him to open his mouth. He didn't. Something hit him on the side of his face and it felt as if his cheekbone had been shattered. He opened his mouth and a duster, tasting of fur as if it had a long nap, was thrust in. Until he frantically worked his tongue, it threatened to slide down his throat to choke him.

He lay across the chair, head stabbed with pain, and saw the larger of the two men leave the room. God Almighty! his mind cried, what was happening? Where had the world that he knew gone?

★   ★   ★

Farnes went down the back stairs and out in the yard, where he swung open the locking bar of the main gates—but did not open the gates until his watch showed that exactly ten minutes had passed since he and Smith had entered the flat. Their timing was perfect. The stolen lorry, carefully chosen not to be visible over the wall, was coming slowly along the road and when Carver, one of the men taken on for muscle rather than for any particular skill, saw the gates being opened, he flicked down the blinkers. The lorry came across and into the yard. The moment the tail was clear, Farnes shut the gates and dropped the locking bar into position. He and Carver, who switched off the engine, waited. They heard nothing to suggest any sort of alarm.

Weir and two others came along the pavement and into the yard by way of the small doorway. Weir said: 'Who's inside?'

'One bloke and his missus,' replied Farnes. 'They're quiet.'

They unlashed the canvas cover, lowered the tailgate, and unloaded all the equipment, then split into two groups, one carrying the gas bottles into the house, the other going, with excavating equipment, down into the cellar. Weir went with Dunder, Ricard, and Carver, to the cellar. This was large and in two parts, one of which had obviously been used at some time to store coal, whilst the second had a large number of worm-eaten, wooden racks against part of one side and a pile of junk in the centre. Weir called for the long linen tape measure and then he and Ricard measured out, from time to time referring to the plan, the point where the tunnel must be started. The light from the single, unshaded bulb was poor and at a quick order from Weir, Carver switched on a large torch which had a wire stand enabling it to be placed in position. The floor of the cellar was made of flagstones, rendered uniformly grey by the dirt of ages and very solidly in position. It took Ricard, as strong as he was in the wrist, several blasphemous minutes before he was able to lever up the first flagstone with the aid of the flat end of a pickaxe. After that there was little difficulty in raising three more.

The earth looked plain dirt-coloured, although the geological maps had shown yellow clay for this area. 'Give us a spade,' said Weir.

Dunder picked up a graft and passed it to Weir, who dug down into the hard-packed soil to bring out a clod some five inches deep: the base of this was yellow clay.

There was only room for one of them to dig, so Carver started and Ricard stood to one side with a second spade to throw the excavated soil well clear. Dunder waited with Weir, ready to give a hand when called upon to do so.

Carver had only dug down a few inches and Weir was impatiently pacing a short section of the flagged floor, well clear of any soil, when suddenly there was a row from upstairs which shocked them so much that they froze, each man holding the position in which he'd been when the noise started. There was a shout, a thudding crash, and a second crash, almost as loud.

Initially, they thought the 'impossible' had happened, the police had broken in and there'd been a short, vicious fight up top. Initially, each man was concerned only with his chances of escape. Then, just as the first of them, Weir, moved, they heard a call.

They recognised Farnes's voice. 'Lofty ... Quick.'

Clearly, whatever had happened, the police had not broken in. Weir raced up the cellar stairs, meeting Farnes at the top.

'Lofty, Shocker's taken a fall.'

Weir's reaction was typical. 'So tell the stupid sod to get up.'

''E's out cold and looks bad.' Farnes wasn't panicking, but there was about him the air of a man who believed something had gone irretrievably wrong. ''E slipped on the stairs and Alf couldn't 'old on to the top end of the bottle. Shocker went flying and it landed on 'im.'

Weir, cursing, climbed the stairs, followed by Farnes. Shocker Turner, their electrical expert, an ugly man with perpetually dripping nose, lay a few feet away from the foot of the next flight of stairs up to the bedrooms, half curled up, his body slightly twisted. His eyes were closed, blood was running out of his nose, and from the side of his mouth, which was open to expose his miscoloured teeth, his complexion was dirty white, and his breathing was uneven.

'Where did he get belted?' demanded Weir.

'In the guts,' said Alf Gates, an Australian, who had been brought in with Carver as the last of the muscle men.

As they stared at him, Turner died.

CHAPTER ELEVEN

From the moment he'd fully regained his senses, Armitage had frantically been listening for the noise of the police rescue. For, of course, there had to be a rescue. There always was. But as time passed, his mind began to conceive the chilling thought that perhaps this wasn't true.

From where he lay, by the side of the chair he'd been sitting in when the men had first broken into the room, he could see Patricia quite clearly. Although she'd managed to work her skirt down a bit, most of her legs was still visible. Her face was twisted with fear, shock, and bewilderment and the sight of her suffering filled him with a mental pain that was as great as his physical pain.

He strained his wrists behind his back to gauge the strength of the bindings and was able to gain just enough movement to make him believe there could be a chance of freeing himself. Then he tried to check on his feet, bringing them up to his hands, but this proved far more difficult.

The hooded Smith—face made brutishly indistinguishable by the nylon—suddenly turned away from the window, where he'd been keeping watch through a gap between curtain and frame, and stared at him, then began to walk across. He wriggled his shoulders as if all he'd been trying to do was to cure an itch. Smith came to a stop, said nothing, but kicked him in the side. The pain was immediate and intense, but not quite intense enough to prevent his wondering, with renewed shocked disbelief, how anyone could inflict violence so casually? After a while, Smith returned to the window.

The pain in his side slowly died down to a steady throb, matching the throb in his head. Had the world gone crazy? he thought wildly. Were these men inhuman?

From beyond the door, but not very far beyond, he heard a shout of alarm. This was followed by a thud which sent a vibration along through the floorboards strong enough for him to feel clearly, then a second thud which produced a slightly lighter vibration. His immediate thought was the police had at last arrived. Smith seemed to be of the same belief because he spun round and stood in a boxer's stance, as if expecting to have to defend himself at any second. When nothing more appeared to happen, Smith crossed to the door and very carefully opened it. As soon as he could see, he opened the door more fully and went outside.

There were no shouts, no more thuds, no other sounds of battle and bitterly Armitage began to accept the fact that after all this could not have been a police rescue. Then he'd got to raise any alarm. Patricia was looking at him and he tried to tell her to start moving towards him, but the gag left him incapable of producing anything but meaningless grunts. He wriggled as quickly as he could, ignoring the added pain, and made progress across the floor until he came within reach of her. He rolled over, so that she could use the tips of her fingers to rip free the tape from his wrists.

Smith looked back into the room, saw what was happening, and raced across. He grabbed Armitage's hair and dragged him free, then kicked him several times, as hard as he could thud his heavy boots home.

* * *

Weir, standing by the end of the table in the dining-room, stared at the other six and saw uncertainty, even hostility, in their expressions. 'I tell you, we get on with the job.'

'It just ain't on,' countered Gates, his Australian accent very marked as it usually was when he got excited or earnest. 'With Shocker dead, we ain't got a chance. Shocker was going to do the alarms.'

There was no escaping the fact. They were a team of experts and muscle men: unlike the muscle men, experts were irreplaceable. Weir, stubbornly, tried to argue round the facts. 'Once we've cut the wires in the conduit under the strong-room floor, there ain't nothing to worry about.'

'Are you joking?' demanded Gates. 'Who's to know now which wires is safe to cut and which isn't: who's to know how to stop triggering off alarms enough to bring the law along on skates?'

They stared at Weir.

Their resistance infuriated him, threatening to set alight his hasty temper, but he had the capacity of being able occasionally—certainly not always—to turn off his anger as if by a switch. He did so now. They were right, yet he wasn't going to let them be right. A man who lost a big job became a figure of derisive amusement: there was no sympathy for failure amongst villains. Somehow, he had to persuade them to continue, even though ... His quick mind began to pick out a solution, but he needed time to check it out and he recognised that it had to be sold to them because it could not be forced on them. And the way to grab them and keep them was to play on their cupidity. 'You'll never get another chance at three million.'

They moved around the room, aimlessly walking from wall to wall, fidgeting with the backs of the chairs, bumping into each other as they turned.

'There's none of you getting less than two

per cent: on three million, that makes sixty grand.'

They'd worked the sums out time and time again but they still now worked them out once more. Burner Aaron, the top expert and on ten per cent, could reach three hundred thousand.

Gates, the sharpest realist amongst them, was the first to break the silence. 'Lofty, it could be a million each, but we can't cut the wires without Shocker.'

Dunder and Carver sat down, their expressions bitter. Gates stared at Weir.

'Don't you like the sound of sixty grand?'

'It's not on,' said Aaron, speaking suddenly.

'Ain't it?' Weir spoke jeeringly. 'Then I guess that's an end to it.'

'Well, is it?'

'You're tellin' me, Burner. You're tellin' me you're dropping three hundred grand.'

'With Shocker dead...'

Weir broke in, mimicking Burner's voice. 'There ain't no way to cut the alarms ... But suppose there is a way?'

They stared at him with renewed intensity, desperately hoping he could prove them wrong.

'Suppose there's a way to keep the job going, despite Shocker being dead?'

'How?' demanded Gates.

'Bringing another electrician in to do the

job.'

'There ain't the time between now and Monday.'

'So we buy time.'

Gates looked at the others to see if they understood, but it was clear that as yet none of them did. 'What d'you mean, Lofty?'

Weir spoke softly. 'We buy time, using the woman. We take her off with us.'

'Do what? You're bleeding daft.'

'For why?'

'What about the bloke? D'you reckon he's going to sit back and just keep quiet?'

'I reckon.' Weir looked at each of them in turn. 'I reckon he will, if he knows that if he opens his mouth to shout, we'll rape his wife stupid, all ways, before ripping her up.'

They were shocked, not by the suggestion, but by the obvious fact that Weir gained a special kind of pleasure from the prospect.

Aaron was the first to speak. 'If we leave 'im on 'is own, 'e could talk easily on account of reckoning the cops'll get us in time to save the woman—then when we come back, the law's waiting. If one of us stays with 'im and the cops come in for any reason, that bloke's for the nick. And maybe the rest of us.' He didn't insult them by spelling out the fact that if the one who stayed was offered a light prison sentence in return for information, he'd possibly sing as hard as he knew how.

Weir said softly: 'Would you call the cops

if you was a civilian and there just wasn't no way of the splits finding where your wife was being held?'

Some of them nodded. Civilians saw things in a very emotional light.

'What 'appens to the woman afterwards?' asked Ricard.

'We kill her,' answered Weir, as if the question was a ridiculous one.

'I don't like it,' said Gates suddenly.

'So if you're that soft, kiss your sixty grand goodbye.'

Gates looked away. Sixty thousand against a woman?

''E could see that's the way we'd 'ave to play it,' objected Dunder. 'So then 'e calls the cops, since things can't get no worse.'

'Lou, can't you see? He's a civilian. He'd never believe we could act so rough. But just in case something goes wrong, we watch the flat. That way, we know if the splits call.'

'How?'

'From the flat across the road what we paid six months' rent for.'

They began to see that the idea was feasible. Weir had shown them how to play it both ways. No civilian husband would dare risk having his wife raped and murdered. But just in case, they'd watch the flat and then if the splits called they'd know the job was blown—but they'd know it without further risk to themselves.

'Where do you keep the woman?' asked Carver.

'At the farm, which we took for three months.'

The isolated farmhouse, at the end of a bleak valley, which they'd rented as a place to gather together and keep all the equipment and the stolen lorry and cars before coming down on this Saturday, offered an ideal place.

'Well?' said Weir softly. He began to massage the soft, satiny skin of his right cheek.

Gates still showed a hesitation. 'It could work, Lofty, only I don't like doing in the woman.'

'Would you rather she had a good butchers at us all so as when we let her go she can have a long heart-to-heart with the splits?'

'Why can't we blindfold 'er on the journey and then...'

'So she listens to our voices and remembers 'em. You talk Aussie. She tells that to the splits. How long after that are you staying outside the nick?'

Gates made no answer.

Farnes, speaking for the first time in a long while, said harshly: 'She's got to be done in.'

Weir said to Gates: 'I won't be asking you to do it, Alf.'

They understood what he intended and felt sorry for the woman, but they were more interested in their percentages of the three

113

million.

Weir knew he now had them with him. 'All right. We stay until Sunday night, like we arranged, 'cause there ain't time to clear up, load the lorry, and get away by daylight. Then, Tony, you and Angel stay in the flat opposite and keep watch. If you see a split near this place, you get on the blower. Right?'

Ricard nodded. 'Sure, Lofty.'

'And when you quit the flat, see there ain't nothing left behind.'

'There won't be,' boasted Carver.

★　　　★　　　★

They had been fed and had been allowed at regular intervals to go along to the bathroom to relieve themselves and in some queer, inverted manner, Patricia and Armitage had come to accept their imprisonment with a degree of equanimity. But such acceptance rested on one unshakable belief—that soon they would be released so they could return to the normal world, the one they'd always lived in, where violence and brutality were things one only read about or saw on the television or cinema screen.

They discovered their mistake early Monday morning, as the church clock struck the half-hour. Farnes, face hidden behind a nylon, came into the room, nodded at Smith,

114

who'd been on guard, and crossed to where Armitage sat, propped up against the side of one of the armchairs. 'We're taking 'er with us and you're staying.'

Armitage stared at him, then began to struggle with his bonds.

'Keep your mouth shut about what's 'appened and she'll be all right. Tell the splits any kind of a story and she'll get raped stupid before we knock 'er off slowly.' Unlike Weir, he spoke in a matter-of-fact voice. For him, this was just a straightforward threat.

Armitage tried to speak.

'We've a contact in the police, what'll tell us if so much as a whisper gets through. One whisper and she's dead—after a time.' Farnes waited a few seconds, then he brought from his pocket a cosh. Using seemingly little effort, he flicked the cosh down and Armitage was blasted into unconsciousness. He stripped off the plaster from Armitage's legs and then crossed to the door and opened it. 'O.K., Lofty.'

Patricia saw a small man with uncovered face come into the room. He stared at her and in his very dark brown eyes there was an expression that, with feminine intuition, she immediately identified. She began to wriggle, to get away from him, but he grabbed her ankles and just for a second caressed them before he ripped off the plaster.

'Get up,' he ordered.

She rolled over on to her side, got on her knees, and stood. The door was open and the doorway seemingly clear. She ran. Carver appeared from the kitchen and blocked the passage. 'Going someplace, lady?' he jeered.

She began to sob, deep sobs which made her body shake.

A tall man came out of the kitchen and pushed past Carver. 'Can't you lay off 'er,' he said.

She identified his accent as Australian and stared at him with mute appeal, but he, as if annoyed that he had spoken, turned aside and went down the passage towards the back stairs.

Weir came out of the sitting-room and stood close to her and there was little difference in their heights. He reached up and took hold of her shoulder and she could feel his fingers moving over her. 'He's back in there with a cord round his neck. It'll be pulled tight if you don't do what you're told.'

She was suddenly far more terrified for Armitage's safety than she was for her own, which meant she had failed to realise that when they let her see their faces they were admitting they had condemned her to death.

CHAPTER TWELVE

Armitage swallowed two more aspirins with the coffee and almost immediately gagged, yet there could be little left in his stomach to vomit. Pain squeezed his head with renewed fire and he closed his eyes and slumped back in the wooden chair.

The fingers of shooting pain gradually eased away, leaving him only a pounding headache and with that he could just about cope. Desperately, he tried to think what to do, but his mind was still scrambled, as if that last blow had knocked all his senses into hopeless confusion. He forced himself to stand up, used the kitchen table to steady himself with, and slowly, like an old man, stepped out into the passage. There'd been a body there—he'd walked round it on the way to the bathroom—lying crumpled half on the cheap, time-dirtied carpet and half on the floorboards. There was dried blood on carpet and floorboards.

He stumbled into the sitting-room and virtually collapsed on to the chair by the telephone. All he had to do was dial 999 and the police would take over. But the men had claimed a contact in the local police who'd warn them. And then Patricia would be raped and murdered.

He looked across the room and his eyes focused and he saw an empty champagne bottle on the drinks cupboard. Patricia and he had finished the last two glasses of champagne with the pudding. It was unbelievable, except it was true, that the normal world could be shattered with such terrifying speed and ruthlessness. He remembered how Patricia had looked, face distorted by fear, as she lay on the floor. What in the name of God had happened to her after he'd been knocked unconscious? Where had they taken her? What was happening to her now?

He had to telephone the police to set in motion her rescue. But if he did that, the mob would immediately learn about the call and Patricia would be appallingly murdered because there was no hope the police could move quickly enough since what could he tell them other than that he'd seen two hooded men, neither of whom he could ever identify? Then he daren't telephone the police. His head pounded more fiercely because of the turmoil in his mind.

Gradually, he recognised he had no option other than to do exactly as they'd ordered him to—nothing. There must be no alarm because then, and only then, would Patricia return, safe, unharmed. So now? He must clear up the blood in order that Amanda, the daily woman, wouldn't notice anything. Check there were no other signs ...

Dudley! How in the hell could he have forgotten Dudley? When he found Patricia was missing he was going to do what any husband would, move heaven and earth to find her.

Armitage groaned. Just when there had seemed to be some chance it suddenly became clear there was none. The men had presumed he and Patricia were husband and wife, a belief he'd deliberately done nothing to destroy because of the consequences of doing so, and their mistaken belief now meant that their demands were quite impossible. If Dudley was told the truth, he'd go straight to the police: if he wasn't told the truth, he'd inevitably go to the police and report his wife missing . . .

His head became a ball of pain and he rested it on his hands. What could a man do when he must take one of two courses and yet either led to disaster? In his mind he saw men without faces ripping the clothes from Patricia, throwing her down on the floor, covering her as she screamed . . .

Time passed. He returned to the sitting-room and here the early sunshine was coming in through the windows to streak the carpet. He took two more aspirins, careless about how many that made. When was Dudley due back? Would he immediately presume her missing? He surely would if he went home before going to the office. So how

119

much time was left in which to reconcile a middle-aged husband to the fact that his young wife was missing, without his rushing round to search for her?

★   ★   ★

Dudley Broadbent had a great respect for the proprieties, one of which was that taxi-drivers did not speak until spoken to. 'No, I did not have a good time,' he snapped. 'And I was working and was not on holiday.'

'Working? In Paris? That's a good story, Guv.'

'I have been in Amsterdam.'

'Is that so? Thought you said Paris. A pal of mine said as how there're a lot of good tit shows there—is that right?'

Broadbent was disgusted by such crudity. The driver decided to charge the sour old bastard extra fare, but after another quick look in the rearview mirror correctly decided that his passenger was not in the market for being suckered.

Easthover House looked time-caressed and peaceful in the sunshine and Broadbent's humour rapidly improved as he felt a warm glow of possession. They drew up in front of the porch, too large and ostentatious in style, and the driver said the fare was ninety pence. Broadbent passed over a pound note and asked for the one penny change, since he

120

believed in tipping an exact ten per cent. The driver, an expression of disbelief on his face, gave him the penny.

Broadbent carried his single suitcase into the house, a little short of breath even though the suitcase wasn't heavy. A late night, he reminded himself. But these days he was often short of breath.

Patricia did not come out into the large hall, even though she must have heard the taxi. It annoyed him because he liked to be greeted on arrival. 'Patricia,' he called out, his voice a shade peevish.

A door banged upstairs and he looked up at the small gallery where a tall, thin, pock-marked woman looked over the carved wooden rail. 'Mornin', Mr. Broadbent,' she said cheerfully. 'Lovely day to come 'ome on. As I said to Bert, it's summer.'

Summer hadn't yet started, astronomically speaking, he thought pedantically. 'Where's Mrs. Broadbent?'

'I wouldn't know. As a matter of fact, I was asking myself the same question earlier on.'

He contained his impatience. 'She must have been here when you arrived?'

'That she wasn't, for I had to let myself in with the spare key. And if you was to ask me, I'd say Mrs. Broadbent ain't been 'ere for quite a bit.'

'Whatever do you mean?'

''Er bed's made up, the dining-room table

121

ain't been used, there's nothing wanting cleaning in the kitchen, and nor's there anything in the washing-up machine.'

'But . . . but if she's gone anywhere, there must be a message?'

'Well, I ain't seen one.'

He began to feel slightly ridiculous, not knowing where his wife was. 'Thank you,' he said, by way of dismissal. She refused to be dismissed and stared down at him with great interest. Muttering angrily, he left his case in the hall and went into the dining-room.

There was nothing on the mantelpiece which was where she usually left any note and he noticed that the cut flowers in the crystal vase were drooping. He left and crossed the hall to the larger of the two sitting-rooms. The Sunday papers were on one of the coffee tables, neatly folded and clearly unread . . . But Patricia always did the *Sunday Telegraph* crossword puzzle.

Still annoyed, but admitting to a little perplexed worry, he went upstairs. The woman was dusting in their bedroom, so he told her he wanted to change and she left. He checked Patricia's nightdress case, shaped like a floppy-eared donkey: the nightdress was inside. In the bathroom, to the left of his changing-room, he found her two toothbrushes were in the small cupboard.

Back in the bedroom, he sat down on one of the tapestry-covered chairs. He was not a fool and work had shown him many times that when a man of middle age—nearly middle age—was married to a woman in her twenties there was often trouble. When he'd married Patricia five years before, many of his friends had probably thought he was setting himself up for a pair of horns. But work had also taught him to judge character and he had judged Patricia to have the kind of sense of duty that would deny any other man the familiarity of her body. She couldn't have gone off with another man. And yet ...

Perhaps her mother was ill. Illness had so dominated her life until the death of her father that she tended to get over-emotional about it. All it needed was for her mother to ring up and say she wasn't feeling too fit and Patricia would get in a panic and rush up to Norwich. Perhaps this had happened and she'd forgotten about his homecoming. Reprehensible, of course, but understandable ... A telephone call to Mrs. Frayne proved she wasn't ill. Worse, it had seemed to him that Mrs. Frayne, a woman for whom he'd never had much affection, had quietly been amused because he didn't know where Patricia was.

He went downstairs where he lit a cigar, even though he normally never smoked before lunch, and he poured out a very early drink.

Amanda Rainer, middle-aged and a spinster though not, village gossip said, a virgin despite her looks, was stupid in a fairly pleasant way and prone to breaking things. She'd infuriated Gwen, but she still only charged twenty pence an hour and Gwen had never been able to replace her. She had a small, rusty car, as angular as herself, and had agreed to come to the flat in Ethington five mornings a week.

There was a crash. She came into the sitting-room. 'I'm afraid I've had a little accident, Mr. Armitage.'

He turned and looked at her.

'It's a cup. Of course, I'll pay for it.' She always offered to pay for breakages, probably because she'd never been asked for the money.

In the odd way in which, when under great emotional stress, a person sometimes concentrated on something entirely immaterial, he noticed that the hair in the mole in the middle of her cheek had grown in length.

'It's the new washing-up liquid: they've made it so slippery. As I said to Doll only yesterday . . .'

He stopped listening. She spoke to him whenever she could because she was simple enough to believe him an important author.

124

He lit another cigarette, even though his mouth tasted foul.

She left, still talking until she'd closed the door behind herself. She hadn't changed, he thought: nothing in the outside world had changed. His terror, pain, and mental agony, were peculiar to himself.

A little while ago, he'd begun to have an idea, but then his thoughts had become all confused again. He tried desperately to concentrate. Dudley was a man who owned things, including his wife. He was pompous, self-satisfied. Wouldn't he surely do anything rather than admit publicly . . .?

The telephone rang.

'Is everything nice and quiet?'

He gripped the receiver more tightly. 'Yes,' he croaked.

'Then I'll tell you something to make you happy. She's fine. Ain't that nice to know?'

He didn't answer.

'I said, ain't that nice to know?'

He realised the caller was gaining pleasure from taunting him. 'Yes.'

'The lads reckon she's great. One of 'em says that with lips like hers, she must be a ripe artist in bed. Is she?'

He shivered.

'Is she?'

'Yes.'

'You don't sound very enthusiastic. Now if you want her back so as you can have more

125

fun together in bed, just keep quiet. 'Cause if you don't we're going to...'

As he listened, he wondered how any mind could be so perverted and sadistic. The man finished speaking and rang off. Armitage found he was shaking.

Amanda Rainer returned to the room. 'I'll be on my way, then, 'cause me and Bertha is going into Cruxton Cross on account of she wants to buy some baby things. It's the fourth one coming and she says she don't know 'ow she'll manage. Like I said, the time to worry about that was eight months ago. Trouble is, Fred likes it too much.'

She had a country person's direct approach towards sex, thought Armitage, in sharp and bitter contrast to the man who'd spoken over the telephone. If he couldn't find a way of keeping Dudley quiet, Patricia would suffer in a manner that ...

CHAPTER THIRTEEN

For the first time in ten years—the waiter had only worked in the club for ten years—Dudley Broadbent refused coffee after his lunch. 'No coffee, sir?' said the waiter, in tones of amazement. Then he hastily pulled himself together. Members of the club were allowed to do anything but bring a lady into the dining-room. He left.

Broadbent's table companion, Epps, said: 'Have you got a real stinker of a case on your hands, Dudley?'

'Eh? What's that?' muttered Broadbent.

'I wondered if you'd a very troublesome case? You've hardly spoken during the meal and just now you quite upset Jim's day by not ordering coffee.'

'Er . . . Yes. Very difficult case.' Broadbent gratefully accepted the proffered excuse. He brought out his cigar case, took out a cigar, cut the end, and lit it. Where was she? He'd telephoned home just before lunch and there'd been no answer. Could she have had some sort of an accident? But then she must have been identified by now. What circumstance could possibly explain her absence, except . . . except the one he refused to consider.

Epps was talking about his nephew, Roger, who'd been a bit wild when young but had now settled down and gained a good two one law degree. Broadbent got up suddenly, thereby cutting off Epps in mid-sentence, and left. Epps watched him leave with dislike, because he'd been going to ask a favour in respect of his nephew.

Down the stairs and on the far side of the lobby was a call-box. Broadbent went into it, switched on the light, brought out the coins in his trousers pocket and stacked them in their denominations, ready for a fairly prolonged call because he was suddenly convinced Patricia would have returned home and he was determined to make it plain, in a dignified way of course, that he'd been very worried and she'd been rather thoughtless. The call was answered, but by the daily woman who worked in the afternoons. She was a miserable, sniffing woman. She said, sniff, Mrs. Broadbent wasn't at home, sniff, that there'd been no messages, sniff, and she wasn't feeling very well so she might not, sniff, be able to stay the whole afternoon.

He picked up the unused coins and replaced them in his pocket, then left the club and walked the four hundred yards to his office. The receptionist smiled a greeting, but he was a trifle frigid in return as he noticed she was still wearing a very short skirt although he'd asked her to wear something more appropriate to a dignified solicitor's office. He went up the first flight of stairs to his office, large and discreetly, but luxuriously, furnished. His middle-aged secretary—in a skirt of decent length—came in and said that two more appointments had been entered in his diary, although she'd had some difficulty in fitting them in because he was so busy. He was a very successful country solicitor. He had a dignified personality, discretion, a touch of servility when dealing with the richer or more influential clients, and three junior partners who were academically clever.

His secretary left. He looked at the telephone, wondering whether to ring again, but then decided it was too soon after his last call. Exerting a great deal of willpower, he resumed work.

*　　　*　　　*

As Armitage turned into Hermione's drive, he was very conscious of the fact that he was gambling everything on his reading of Broadbent's character: yet it was a gamble he had to take.

He knocked on the front door and when there was no immediate answer he suddenly realised for the first time that she might be out. It was a frightening thought. He rang again and kept his finger on the bell-push.

The door was eventually opened by the daily woman who said she was very sorry, but she and Miss Grant had been up in one of the attic rooms, clearing out some things. He asked if he might have a word with Miss Grant and the woman showed him into the sitting-room.

He picked up a copy of *The Field* and leafed through the pages, but wasn't conscious of anything he looked at. All the time his mind pictured the things the man said they'd do to Patricia if the alarm was given . . .

'What brings the great author here in the middle of a working afternoon?' Hermione was dressed in slacks and a sweater which might just have suited a woman half her age and size. She studied him. 'My God! You look as though you've been burning the candle in the middle as well as at both ends.'

He was grateful for the lead-in. 'Well, as a matter of fact . . .' He stopped. The more she guessed at what he was going to say, the more readily she would believe what he told her.

'Something's going on!' She slumped down on one of the beautiful leather armchairs and stared at him with bright, inquisitive eyes.

'Well, I . . . I've come to see if you'll help me.'

'What is it—something to do with you and Pat?'

He fiddled with one of the buttons of his well-worn sports jacket. 'Yes, it is.'

'Then you don't surprise me,' she said, with satisfaction. Yet there was a hint of something else in her expression: a touch of bitter sadness. 'For God's sake, stop drooping like the Tower of Pisa and sit down before you collapse.'

He sat down.

'Will you have a drink?'

'Yes, I'd like one.'

'You're someone after my own heart, George. No bloody nonsense about the sun

130

being over the yardarm. If I want a drink in the afternoon, I want one. But Dudley ...' She'd introduced the name deliberately and she stared more fixedly at him to note his reaction.

'What I've come about concerns Dudley as well.'

'I thought it probably did. But get the drinks before telling me the plot. I'll have a gin and tonic.'

He poured out two gin and tonics, though he'd seldom wanted a drink less. When he handed her a glass, he said abruptly: 'You know Patricia and I have been seeing quite a bit of each other?'

'Of course I do. Damn it, she always used me to pull the wool over Dudley's eyes.'

'You've been very kind.'

'How in the hell she ever came to marry him, I can't imagine: she might as well have married a maiden aunt.'

'When Pat came to dinner on Saturday, we ... we got to talking about what we were going to do. It's a hell of a situation.'

'Happens every day of the week and if a middle-aged man is fool enough to marry someone half his age, he ought to expect it.' She spoke with open satisfaction.

'It's not that easy.'

'How d'you mean?'

'You know Pat—she's got a conscience a mile high. Because of that, she wouldn't burn her bridges and ... even though she admitted she really wanted to ... You won't tell anyone what I'm telling you?'

'Good God, no!'

'Thanks. In the end she was so mixed up she said she had to get away and think things over entirely on her own. So she left on Sunday.'

'On Sunday!'

He shook his head. 'We slept in different bedrooms.'

Hermione spoke almost angrily. 'My God! You're as bad as she is.'

He tried to smile. 'It certainly wasn't my fault ... She begged me not to tell Dudley anything in case she decides she must stick with him and she doesn't want him hurt.'

'Nobody else could be so soft as to think of Dudley at such a time.'

'But I had to promise her I wouldn't do anything precipitate.'

'It strikes me that if you'd done something precipitate the whole thing would be sorted out by now.'

Hermione shook her head as if she couldn't understand. She finished her drink.

'Look, will you get on to Dudley and say that one of your mutual old school friends suddenly turned up on a motoring holiday and she suggested Pat went with her and Pat suddenly decided to take a holiday, knowing Dudley wouldn't mind.'

'But she'd know Dudley would think she'd gone quite crazy to do a thing like that without reference to him.'

'Perhaps, but it'll keep him quiet just long enough for her to make up her mind what she's going to do. Then if she decides to come to me, it won't make things worse if he learns she lied about things, while if ... if she decides to stick with him, she'll surely be able to persuade him she was telling the truth.'

'It's obvious which of you two thought up something that tortuous!' She lit a cigarette.

Dudley would force himself to believe the story, thought Armitage. But he'd know he was forcing himself, and why. Which was why he wouldn't actually check up on the story, because to do so might be to learn it was a lie and then he'd have to acknowledge the fact that she'd almost certainly gone off with another man and with his character he'd rather do anything than that.

           ★   ★   ★

Dudley was considering what advice to give to the beneficiaries of a trust fund now worth approximately a quarter of a million pounds when his telephone buzzed once. Miss Grant wanted to speak to him. He began to tap on the desk with his fingers. He certainly didn't want to talk to Hermione Grant. He thought her a horrible woman, rude of tongue and manner, perhaps a lesbian, and he had done his best to break up the friendship between her and Patricia. She knew this and she knew why he did it and she hated him for it.

'Dudley? It's taken a bloody long time to get through to you. Some silly bitch said you'd given orders you weren't taking any calls.'

He hated to hear a woman swear. 'I am very busy,' he said curtly.

'Too busy to hear about Patricia?'

He suddenly found himself short of breath. 'What do you mean?'

'She's not at your place, is she? She came and spent part of Saturday with me.'

He sweated profusely. What was she going to tell him? His hand, holding the telephone, shook. 'Well?' His voice was croaky.

'Whilst she was with me, June turned up.'

'Who?'

'June Havering. She was June Burn, before she got married.'

'Who is this woman? Why can't you tell me what happened?'

'We were at school together and June and Pat were as thick as thieves. You know what I mean?'

She'd managed to make even that sound obscene. 'Go on,' he muttered.

'June's a grass widow for a month and has been motoring around the country and when she heard Pat was also a grass widow she suggested Pat went along with her for a while.'

'Pat was not a grass widow,' he snapped.

'She was on Saturday. So she went off in the early afternoon.'

'Are you telling me she left with this woman on a motoring tour? But she knew perfectly well I was coming back today.'

'What's the matter? She's not going to be away very long.'

'She should have telephoned me. I gave her the number of my hotel.'

'And have you get all pompous and tell her she couldn't go?'

He had never sworn at a woman, but he nearly swore at her then. 'Where is she now? How can I get hold of her?'

'You can't. They can be anywhere between here and South Wales.'

'I see. Thank you for telling me.' Not even now did he forget his manners 'Goodbye.' He replaced the receiver.

He stared down at the papers on his desk. To have acted like that was quite contrary to Patricia's nature. Could she really have just driven off, without any reference to him, knowing he'd be back on the Monday? Yet Hermione had said that's what she'd done. And the alternative to believing Hermione's story was ... And as Armitage had foreseen, he was not prepared to consider the alternative, because to do so was to expose

135

himself to the possibility of ridicule and hurt.

He must make it quite clear to Patricia when she returned, he very deliberately and carefully thought, that her inconsiderate actions had been most thoughtless and caused him considerable distress.

★   ★   ★

Hermione said: 'He swallowed it, hook, line, and sinker.'

Armitage tried not to show the intensity of the relief he felt.

'The man's a bloody fool.'

Strangely, Armitage felt sympathy for Dudley now.

'So you can tell Pat she's quite in the clear. And also tell her from me to worry about what she wants for a change, and not what other people want.'

Armitage felt light-headed. The desperate gamble had paid off. Dudley was silenced and there would be no alarm over Patricia's disappearance.

CHAPTER FOURTEEN

The council car-park in Ayrton Road—like all those in Ethington—worked on the honour system with a motorist expected to put a five-or a ten-pence piece in the ticket machine and then to display the ticket in the windscreen. Honour being a doubtful starter in the modern world, the council employed a full-time inspector to check up on all the cars in the car-parks and to note the numbers of cars showing no ticket or a ticket out of time. When a car was parked for several days a report was also put through to the police by the inspector because from time to time abandoned stolen cars were left in the car-parks.

*　　*　　*

Police Constable Steel, seconded to the C.I.D. for six months as aide, was imaginative, ambitious, and very eager to do sufficiently well to be selected for training and posting as detective constable. But to his chagrin, however, he seemed to be given little to do but routine, boring paperwork so that if the opportunity arose to do something more constructive he became very enthusiastic indeed.

The report came through of a Morris 1300 which had been in the Ayrton Road car-park since Saturday evening. He checked the number with the latest lists of stolen cars and found it was not recorded, then went along to the D.I's room. French was out. Steel hesitated only briefly, took the bunch of

137

British Leyland master keys from the small, old-fashioned safe, signed the notebook to say he'd taken them, and left the station to walk to Ayrton Road.

The Morris had none of the possible signs of having been stolen for a joy-ride and then abandoned—dirty, slashed seats, broken instrument panel, stolen transistor. The doors were locked and he unlocked them, careful that in doing so he touched no surface that was capable of recording a fingerprint. Inside, he found no means of identification and nothing beyond a paper bag, bearing the name of Gwelf Supermarket. He opened the bag. There was a jar of baby beets, which he liked, and a slice of pressed beef, which he didn't because it was all too frequently on the menu at the canteen. The pressed beef was clearly on the way to going bad. He replaced the bag, relocked the car, and returned to the station.

French was back, in his office, and he listened with gentle cynicism to Steel's report and wondered how much longer it would be before Steel ceased to see a criminal behind every lamp-post?

'But the pressed beef, sir—going bad. That means someone was buying for a meal but got interrupted.'

French scratched his ear. Someone had bought the food, presumably for consumption over the week-end, but instead of putting it in a fridge had left it in the car and the car in the car-park. By definition, that was to suggest something unusual had happened.

'I think it ought to be checked,' said Steel.

French finally nodded. For once there wasn't much of importance in hand. That was, other than the still unsolved murder of Healey. And even Connell was beginning to accept the fact that with so few leads it was likely to remain unsolved.

Steel went through to the C.I.D. general room, telephoned the vehicle department at county hall, and asked for a check-out on the car number he gave. Was it priority? He hesitated just long enough for the man on the other end of the line to say that it was much too late in the day to do anything now and would he please forward the request in writing on Form J62?

Tomorrow, he thought, he'd ring again and since he'd speak to a different clerk he'd say at the beginning it was priority. He was young, but he was quick to learn.

★   ★   ★

Armitage awoke and stared up at the ceiling, vaguely outlined as the growing daylight reached through the curtains.

Were they carrying out their promise and not harming Patricia? No one had the

139

slightest idea she'd been kidnapped, not even her own husband. When would they come back? At the week-end? He hoped to God it would be then because Dudley would only keep quiet for a certain length of time. After that he'd have to begin to believe the worst.

When he thought how close a thing it had been, keeping the news from Dudley, he felt slightly sick. Patricia's life had rested on a very thin strand. But the strand had held and she was going to be safe. He repeated that as if it were a prayer. She was going to be safe.

*   *   *

French was silently swearing as he read a circular letter from county H.Q. when Steel came into his room. He dropped the offending circular on to the desk.

'Sorry to bother you, sir, it's about the car in Ayrton Road car-park.'

French reached in his pocket for a pack of cigarettes and then remembered he'd smoked his last cigarette twenty minutes ago. 'Give me a fag, lad.'

Steel passed across a pack of cigarettes. 'I've learned it belongs to a Mrs. Broadbent who lives at Easthover House in Weldersham. The name seems vaguely familiar.'

'It'd be a sight more familiar if you'd much to do with the courts. Her bastard of a husband springs more motorists—provided they can afford his fees—than the rest of the mouthpieces put together.' French spoke without much rancour. It was a lawyer's job to get a guilty client brought in not guilty.

'I telephoned the house and had a word with the daily woman. She says Mrs. Broadbent apparently unexpectedly went on a motoring holiday and left early Saturday afternoon. But according to the parking ticket in the car it was parked there at five-fifty-eight.'

'What kind of motoring holiday since she didn't go in her own car?'

'The woman wasn't very certain as she'd only heard it all from Mr. Broadbent, but Mrs. Broadbent was visiting a Miss Grant when an old school friend turned up and suggested the holiday and Mrs. Broadbent went off.'

'Just like that?'

'So the woman was told. Apparently, Mr. Broadbent went on and on about how much his wife had liked this person at school. She said it was a bit odd the way he talked because usually he doesn't say much to her except good morning or goodbye.'

'You seem to have got a good lot out of the woman.'

Steel looked pleased.

French picked up a pencil and began to doodle on the edge of the circular. 'It probably doesn't add up to a row of beans.'

Steel spoke eagerly. 'But there's the meat, bought after she's supposed to have gone on the holiday, the fact her husband is suddenly very talkative, the fact her trip was so unexpected.'

French looked up. 'So what are you suggesting?'

Steel coloured, because he hadn't the nerve to put into words the solution his mind had conceived.

'You know,' said French quietly, 'if I was asked to name the man least likely to bump off his wife, I'd start thinking of Dudley Broadbent.'

Steel fidgeted with his coat. 'But don't you think it's a bit odd, sir?'

French put down the pencil. If the wife had left in the afternoon how had she, assuming it was she, gone shopping in the car in the early evening? Why was the car left in the car-park? Why was the food left in the car? If her husband had been using the car, how had he got home? Why should he leave it in the car-park over the week-end?

'Should I have a word with Mr. Broadbent?' asked Steel.

'It'll be better if I do.'

Steel looked disappointed.

'Listen, lad,' said French in kindly fashion, 'in the little puddle of Ethington, Broadbent is a big frog. If you handled him as you did the last person I sent you to question, he'd have your guts for garters.'

Steel looked annoyed and tried to explain how that had not been his fault, but French shut him up.

★　　★　　★

Broadbent's secretary came in and said that Detective Inspector French would be very grateful if he might have a word. Broadbent looked at his watch. 'All right. But tell the man I can't give him much time.'

He began to read through some papers and when the detective inspector came in he gave only the briefest of acknowledgements, then resumed reading. French showed no resentment at this incivility.

Broadbent finally pushed the papers to one side. 'Well—what is the trouble?'

'As a matter of fact, sir, the person I really wanted to have a word with was Mrs. Broadbent, but I understand she's not at home?'

'How d'you know that?' Broadbent's voice was sharp.

'I phoned your house earlier and a woman told me.'

'Why d'you want to speak to my wife?' Broadbent felt tension grip him, because he was certain he was going to learn something which at all costs he didn't want to learn.

'It's in connexion with her car.'

Broadbent relaxed, opened the heavily chased silver cigarette case on his desk, took from it a cigarette, and pushed it across. French got up and helped himself to a cigarette. He then flicked open his lighter for both of them, before resuming his seat. 'There's been a hit-and-run accident, which could prove fatal, and we've an eyewitness who says he identified the driver as Mrs. Broadbent.'

'Preposterous rubbish!' snapped Broadbent. 'When was this accident?'

'Sunday morning, at ten thirty-four.'

'At that time my wife was a great many miles from here.'

'Of course, I know that if Mrs. Broadbent had unfortunately had an accident, she'd have instantly reported it, but I had to check.'

'Naturally,' agreed Broadbent, but resentfully, as if it was so obvious that that check was totally unnecessary.

'I think, though, I must get a formal statement from Mrs. Broadbent. You know how it is when you get so positive a witness statement? Perhaps you can tell me something—where was her car at the time of the accident?'

'Sunday morning? At Miss Grant's, I suppose.'

'You suppose?'

'Damn it, Inspector, what are you suggesting?'

'I'm not suggesting anything, sir.'

'My wife was visiting Miss Grant when this old friend of hers arrived and suggested going for a short motoring holiday. I therefore logically presume the car's at Miss Grant's.'

'Well, the quickest way to deal with the matter until your wife returns is to go and have a check on the car and see it's undamaged ... Will you give me Miss Grant's address?'

Broadbent said: 'Broughton Hall, Madresfield.'

French stood up. 'Thanks very much and I'm sorry to have interrupted you ... By the way, sir, do you like pressed beef and pickled baby beetroot?'

Broadbent tried to understand the reason for the question. 'Yes,' he said finally, 'I like them very much.'

★   ★   ★

Hermione Grant was weeding a flower-bed, watched from a distance by a glowering gardener, when a battered Vauxhall drove in. A man, tallish, greying hair, a craggy-looking face, climbed out and spoke to her. 'Miss Grant?'

She studied him. 'Yes?'

'My name is Detective Inspector French.'

'What d'you want?'

He was untroubled by her curtness. 'Just to

145

ask you a question or two.'

She rubbed her hands together to knock off the earth on them and then led the way into the house, changing in the hall from gardening shoes into worn-out, slopping slippers. In the sitting-room she went straight over to the cocktail cabinet. 'What d'you drink?' she demanded.

'Have you a light ale?'

'No. I don't like the stuff: puts too much gas inside one.'

There was a quick chuckle. 'Then perhaps a Cinzano?'

She poured out a large Cinzano and a whisky and soda, passed over the Cinzano, flopped down in one of the armchairs, and drank. 'Well? What's got you running here?'

He told her about the hit-and-run accident and the eyewitness and how a quick check on Mrs. Broadbent's car would make a liar out of the eyewitness.

Hermione lit a cigarette. 'All very interesting. But what's it to do with me?'

'I understood Mrs. Broadbent's car was here?'

'Understood it from whom? Why on earth should it be here?'

'Didn't she leave it here when she went off with an old school friend of hers, a Mrs. Havering?'

Hermione drew on the cigarette as she tried, and failed, to see some way out of the

146

situation. 'All I know is, she said she'd like to go with June on the trip and she'd drive home to get some clothes and things. Surely her car's at her place?'

'Mr. Broadbent says not.'

'Then obviously, for some reason, she left it somewhere else. Probably at a garage, for servicing.'

'Which is her garage?'

'How the hell should I know?' She drank quickly. The story which had been concocted to fool Dudley was proving, under sterner questioning, to be as full of holes as a colander.

French said: 'I think, the circumstances being what they are, the only thing to do is to get in touch with Mrs. Havering's home and see if they've any idea where she is.'

'I haven't the address.'

French showed only the mildest surprise. 'That may not matter too much if she's a member of an old girls' association. What's the name of the school you all went to?'

Hermione stubbed out the cigarette, stood up, and crossed to the cocktail cabinet to pour herself out another drink.

★   ★   ★

Armitage stared at Hermione and felt as if something were squeezing his guts with ice. That bloody car! How could he have forgotten it?

'Has she had a car accident?' asked Hermione.

'Of course not.' He crossed the sitting-room and stared down at the High Street, becoming busy as people returned home at the end of the working day. 'It was just the detective playing a double game. Patricia left her car somewhere near here and the police are curious. They'll have been to Dudley and he'll have told them about the motoring holiday.'

Hermione's eyes were beady. 'The car's been parked near here ever since Saturday night?'

'Well?' he replied shortly. He turned round.

'So Patricia's been here all the time?'

He shook his head. 'No.'

She spoke impatiently. 'Come on, George, you can tell me the truth.'

'I told you the truth. She left here on Sunday morning.'

'You don't think I'm going to believe that? Leave her car out in the open when she was going away for days? After being married to Dudley for God knows how many years?'

'She was . . . too disturbed to think clearly.'

She leaned forward. 'Why won't you tell me the truth?'

'I am,' he said desperately. 'She left here Sunday morning and went up to London by

148

train.'

She stared at him with an expression of growing anger, but he was too busy trying frantically to find a way out of the maze to notice it. After several seconds she stood up. 'I'm not going to stay if you refuse to trust me,' she said petulantly.

His relief at her going was all too obvious.

'I'm very hurt. Very hurt, indeed, after all I've done for you.' She left, hurrying down the stairs and almost falling. She refused to say goodbye.

CHAPTER FIFTEEN

The bell rang and Armitage went down the stairs to open the front door of the flat and he faced a man who smiled politely and spoke quietly and pleasantly. 'My name's Detective Inspector French.' He showed his warrant card. 'Have you time for a quick word?'

Armitage tried to sound casually astonished and failed. 'What brings you here? . . . Sure, come on in.'

French stepped inside and although he didn't appear to be examining Armitage closely, he missed none of the signs of nervous strain and tension.

Armitage led the way upstairs and, once they were in the sitting-room and seated,

French said: 'I've been talking to Miss Grant a second time, following a telephone call to Mrs. Havering, and she now says you'll be able to help. I'm trying to have a word with Mrs. Broadbent, but unfortunately no one seems to know exactly where she is.'

Surprisingly, it took several seconds for Armitage to realise that Hermione must have deliberately given his name. Wildly, he wondered why? Then he remembered the look in her eyes when she'd left, only a short time ago, and he knew she was getting her own back on him because he'd refused to confide in her.

'Can you tell me where Mrs. Broadbent is?'

He tried to think clearly, and couldn't, because his mind was panicking from the knowledge of what would happen to Patricia if this detective learned the truth.

'Mr. Armitage,' said French, 'do you understand what I'm saying?'

'I ... I'm sorry.' He passed the back of his hand over his forehead. 'I haven't been very well recently.'

'I'm sorry to hear that,' replied French. 'Then I'll worry you for as little time as possible ... Now, as I understand Miss Grant, you asked her to tell Mr. Broadbent that his wife had gone on a motoring holiday?'

The question was so quietly put and French so pleasant that Armitage began to think he might talk himself out of even the present crisis. 'Yes.'

'It seems a bit odd, so will you tell me why?'

'How . . . how far is all this going to go?'

'Only as far as it needs to, Mr. Armitage.'

'But what about her husband?'

French rubbed his square chin. 'At the moment I can't say any more than that Mr. Broadbent has not reported his wife as missing or requested us to search for her. If he does, we'll have to tell him what we know. Until then, it depends on what you have to say to me now.'

Armitage told him the same story he'd told Hermione and French made a few notes. Patricia had stayed Saturday night, in the spare bedroom, and on Sunday morning had been so mentally upset that she'd decided to go off on her own. She'd taken a train to London and had refused to say where she was going to stay in case he tried to get in touch with her. As soon as she knew her own mind and what she was going to do, she'd return.

French looked up from his notebook. 'So there really is no way I can get hold of her right away?'

'I'm afraid there isn't.' Armitage was certain the story had been believed because of French's continuing easy manner.

'But you've some idea of how long she's gone for?'

'She did say she reckoned to be back within the week.'

French dropped his notebook in his pocket, then said: 'She must have had some things with her, I suppose? Clean clothes, toilet articles, that sort of thing?'

It was absurd to suggest Patricia would have gone away for a week without them. 'Yes.'

'Right. Well, that's all, thanks very much ... By the way, I read one of your books some time back and quite enjoyed it.'

Armitage muttered something suitable, as his mind began to play back all he'd said, to convince himself the secret was safe.

* * *

Carver had never been so bored. For him, life was lights, booze, and women, yet now life was watching a flat, twelve hours in every twenty-four. Just as soon as he could, he decided, he'd go down to Nestor, where Weir had told him to buy all their grub, and he'd get a bit of fresh air, buy a paper to find out if Warrington had won their rugby match the previous night, and see if there were any magazines with girls. He'd forgotten what girls looked like.

Across the road, a man walked up to the door of the flat and checked the number. Carver immediately placed him as a split, even though he'd have been unable to say exactly to what details his inbuilt alarm had reacted. He watched through the binoculars. The man rang the bell, Armitage opened the door, and the man showed something—his warrant card?—then the two of them went inside.

Carver hurried into the nearest bedroom and shook the snoring Ricard awake. 'Tony, there's a split gone in.'

Ricard took a few seconds to awaken sufficiently fully to understand the import of the words. 'D'you say just one?'

'Yeah.'

'If they've got the news, they won't send just one.'

'Come and have a butchers.'

Ricard climbed out of bed on which there was just a blanket and pulled on trousers and sweater over his T-shirt and pants. He followed Carver into the other room.

Through binoculars it was possible to see the front half of the sitting-room and the chair in which the man was seated. From time to time he wrote in what looked to be a regulation-size notebook. Ricard swore violently. He swung the binoculars round to look into the bank. There, everything was normal, with not another split in sight. Yet if Armitage had grassed, the place would be full of them. If he hadn't grassed, what was a split doing in this place? The problem was too

153

subtle for Ricard to solve. 'I'm getting on to the blower to Lofty.'

★   ★   ★

Because Weir could never readily acknowledge himself to be wrong, his instinct was to disbelieve Tony Ricard. The man in the flat had been writing in a regulation-size notebook. How the hell could Ricard accurately judge the size from across the street? So Carver agreed the man had been a split. Neither of them was a genius. The man might have been a reporter, doing a piece for the local rag, or someone carrying out a survey ... But Ricard and Carver weren't fools and if they judged the man a split, there was a very good chance they were right.

Aaron and Smith watched him, their expressions similar. They believed the job had been blown. But, Weir told himself, it couldn't be.

Aaron put his thoughts into words. 'The job's over.'

'No,' snapped Weir vehemently.

'Lofty, it ain't no good. With the splits around, it's finished.'

Weir's instinct was to curse wildly, but he managed to control his temper because only reasoned argument was going to alter Aaron's mind. 'If the job was blown, there'd be an army of splits, not just one.'

'Maybe there was an army, only Tony and Angel didn't see 'em,' said Aaron flatly.

'They swear there couldn't be.'

Aaron shook his head.

'Are you giving up, then, just like that? Kicking three million quid down the cawsy?'

Aaron hesitated, then said: 'There ain't no way of making sure.'

'Yes, there is,' answered Weir.

After a while, almost reluctantly, Aaron said: 'How?'

'Her.' Weir jerked his head towards the beamed ceiling.

★   ★   ★

Simply because it wasn't possible to stay utterly and totally frightened for days, Patricia had begun to regain hope. They'd promised she'd go free when the robbery was successfully carried out and that George wouldn't be hurt. The man who was reasonably pleasant to her, an Australian, had reassured her several times. And on top of that, despite her outwardly quiet nature, she had great courage and will-power.

She was talking to Gates about Australia, and he was trying to shock her with some of the broader slang, when they heard the key in the door. He stopped in mid-sentence and they both turned. The door opened and Farnes came in. 'You're wanted,' he said to

Patricia, and jerked his head.

This was the first time such a thing had happened—she'd never left the room except to go to the bathroom—and she was immediately apprehensive. Instinctively, she looked to Gates for help, but he carefully made it clear he would give none.

'Come on, lady,' said Farnes impatiently.

She slid off the bed, stood up, and smoothed down her dress, although it had become so crumpled that nothing she could do would really neaten it. She could smell herself, not having had a bath or proper wash in days, and this was yet one more humiliation. But she found the courage to demand: 'What's the matter?'

'Lofty wants you downstairs.'

'Why?'

'Lady, stop arguing.'

She left the room. Farnes frightened her in a straightforward manner—unlike Weir—because she sensed that he knew no humanity.

They went down stone stairs with a half-turn and into a squarish room with two bay windows. Weir was telephoning and when he looked at her she audibly gasped because his face was so thick with hatred. Two other men were present, but they stared at her with expressions she couldn't read.

Weir spoke into the phone. 'Who the bleeding hell ... I'm telling you, you had a

156

split ... A detective, you stupid bastard. I told you what we'd do ... Husband? Whose husband?' Weir turned to face Patricia. 'Who's your husband?'

Farnes, Aaron, and Smith showed their complete surprise at the question.

Patricia hesitated.

'Who's your husband, you stupid bitch? Ain't he Armitage?'

She shook her head.

He cursed her and although none of the words were new to her, they took on new and twisted meanings because of his viciousness.

Weir spoke into the phone again. 'What d'you tell the split? ... What else? ... What did he say? ... Nothing else? ... Then you listen and just keep on listening.' Weir nodded at Farnes and then put down the receiver.

Farnes grabbed both her hands from behind and wrenched them round her back and forced them up until she stood on tiptoe to try to ease the pain. He jerked her forward until she was immediately in front of Weir.

Weir spoke to her, his voice thin. 'Your boy friend's had a visitor. A bleeding split, wondering where you've got to. Your boy friend sent him away with a story, but just to make certain he keeps talking right, he's going to listen to a bit of what'll happen if he don't.'

Weir grabbed the front of her dress and

157

ripped it open. She began to struggle, but Farnes applied more pressure to her arms and she had to stop. Weir tore her petticoat down, then wrenched at the brassière, but couldn't break it. He took a flick knife from his pocket, freed the blade, and sliced through the material connecting the two cups.

He fondled her breasts. She closed her eyes. Then he gripped each nipple between thumb and forefinger and twisted fiercely in opposite directions and her eyes jerked open as she screamed violently.

CHAPTER SIXTEEN

It was hours now, since Armitage had heard the screams over the telephone, yet they still echoed through his mind. He poured himself another drink.

He'd pleaded, promised anything and everything, if only they'd stop, but the screams had continued until the sweat had rolled down his face.

He finished the drink, but couldn't silence the screams.

★   ★   ★

The weather had done a turn-about as a cold, easterly wind brought back thick grey-bellied

158

clouds. French, wishing he'd put on the sweater his wife had suggested before he left that morning, climbed out of his car and stared at Easthover House. It was nice to be rich, he thought, with only a twinge of envy.

He rang the bell and eventually Broadbent opened the door. He was full of pompous annoyance. What was a policemen doing interrupting him this early in the morning . . .

'I'm a litte worried about your wife,' said French.

Broadbent abruptly looked away.

He hadn't been asked in, but French entered and shut the door. The hall, tastefully furnished, was warm and he guessed the central heating was set at at least seventy: easy when one didn't have to worry about fuel bills. 'I rang Mrs. Havering yesterday,' said French.

Broadbent's fury, based on fright, was immediate. 'Who the devil said you could?'

There were some jobs French hated, and this was one of them. 'Mrs. Havering told me that she has not left home in weeks, far less been on any motoring holiday.'

Broadbent seemed to shrink a little. 'I don't believe it,' he muttered. 'It's impossible. You spoke to the wrong Mrs. Havering.'

'No, sir. She was June Burn before she married and when at school was a close friend of your wife.'

'Then ... then I understood the wrong name.'

French waited.

'My wife ... My wife's not with another man,' said Broadbent suddenly. His voice rose. 'You've got to understand that.'

'My latest information is that she's gone up to London, on her own, but I've no idea where.'

'You said on her own?'

'Yes, sir.'

Broadbent took a handkerchief from his pocket and mopped his brow. He was suddenly looking very middle-aged.

'What I'd like to know now, Mr. Broadbent, is whether you've any idea where she might have gone? Are there any hotels in which you normally stay when you go to London?'

Broadbent named two.

'Can you tell me how many clothes you think she took with her? This would give an idea of how long she intends to be away.'

'I ... I don't think she's taken any clothes,' said Broadbent, very slowly.

As he'd checked, wondered French, how could he have made himself believe she'd gone on a motoring holiday? 'What about toilet articles? Toothbrush?'

Broadbent shook his head.

'If she has a bank account of her own, would you give me the name of the bank and

160

an authorisation to check it?'

French wondered whether Broadbent yet understood where his questions were really leading, or whether he was still fighting his growing belief that his wife must have run off with another man?

★   ★   ★

Armitage drained the glass, hesitated, then poured himself out another whisky. He noticed that the bottle was now almost empty. He heard the doorbell ring and it seemed to take on the shrill violence of a scream. He ignored it, but it rang again and when he finally went down he found his caller was Detective Inspector French and a younger man.

'I'd like a word or two more with you,' said French. It was as much a demand as anything.

Bitterly, Armitage stepped aside for them to enter and then led the way upstairs. Tell them the truth and they'd drop everything to help: tell them the truth and Patricia's screams would be multiplied a thousandfold before she died.

'This is Detective Constable Steel,' said French, by way of a brief introduction, just before they all sat. Armitage noticed that Steel was looking at the drink by his side. It was still early enough in the morning to make it noteworthy.

'Mr. Armitage, will you describe again what happened when Mrs. Broadbent came here on Saturday?'

He told them, speaking slowly enough to check everything before he said it so that there should be no discrepancies with what he'd said last time.

'I don't think you've ever actually said how Mrs. Broadbent went to London?' said French.

'I think I did. By train.'

'How did she get to the station?'

'I drove her in my car.'

'So what happened to her car?'

'She left it parked near here. As you well know.'

French looked slightly nonplussed, as if he'd been hoping to trip up Armitage.

Armitage began to think that all the stories about country bumpkin police must be true. 'What's all the mystery about?' he demanded, taking the offensive.

'There's no mystery and all we really want to do is to have a word or two with Mrs. Broadbent as soon as possible.'

'That won't be for a week.'

'But are you sure it won't be longer? Could she have taken clothes for more than a week, d'you think?'

'No.'

'How many suitcases did she have?'

Armitage answered carelessly: 'Just the one.'

'In which she'd have had her night clothes, spare underclothes, toilet articles, and so on?'

'Of course. What else would she have been carrying?'

'It rather interests me. Her husband has checked and no suitcase is missing from her home, none of her night clothes are gone, and all her toilet things are still in her bathroom.'

Armitage was shocked to discover the bumpkin of a country detective had tricked him.

'It doesn't seem reasonable,' continued French, in the same level voice, 'that any woman would go away for a week's stay without night clothes, toilet articles, and spare underclothes, at the very least.'

There was a silence.

'Do you like pressed beef?' asked French.

Armitage stared at him with uneasy surprise. Finally, he said: 'No.'

French sighed. 'Will you tell me the truth now? Is Mrs. Broadbent in this flat, hiding from her husband?'

'Of course not.'

'Then would you have any objection to my searching it quickly?'

He had to keep the detectives away. 'I'd object strongly.'

'Why?'

'It's a matter of privacy.'

French shrugged his shoulders. 'You've been cleaning the hall carpet recently?'

Armitage could not hide the shock that that question occasioned. All too clearly, he remembered the dead man and the blood which had spilled over the carpet and the floorboards. Cleaning the carpet had left a circle where the colours were fresher. 'I stupidly spilt a pot of jam over it.'

'Jam?' repeated French heavily. 'I will put a previous question to you again. Do you mind if we make a search of your flat?'

'The answer's the same,' Armitage replied hoarsely.

'You'll force me to get a search warrant.'

Armitage said nothing.

French stood up and D.C. Steel followed suit, opened notebook still in his right hand. 'Have you anything you'd like to add to what you've said, Mr. Armitage, or would you like to amend any of your statements?'

He was so bloody polite about it all. Armitage's mind raced on. Was there anything they could find if they searched? Surely there could be no traces of blood left? He'd scrubbed the floorboards and cleaned the carpet again and again. 'Nothing,' he said.

French led the way out of the room.

*   *   *

For once, Hermione was wearing an expensive frock, made for her, but somehow she'd deprived it of all reasonable shape and as she stood in the centre of Armitage's sitting-room she looked as ill dressed as ever. 'Why won't you tell me, George? Why won't you trust me?' She was speaking in bewildered tones, but anger was very close.

Armitage answered wearily: 'I keep telling you the truth. I don't know where Pat is.'

'And I don't believe you.' She crossed to one of the chairs and thumped herself down in it. 'I'm not going until you tell me.'

Her overriding emotion was, he belatedly realised, a twisted jealousy. It was that which had made her betray him to the police. 'Hermione, I swear I trust you completely. If I knew where Pat was, I'd tell you.'

'You're lying.' She opened her handbag and brought out a cigarette case. He offered her cigarettes and with childish ill manners she ignored him and took one of her own and lit it. 'You know perfectly well where Patricia is and it's wicked of you not to tell me. Look how I helped you both. You used to trust me then—when you wanted something from me. It was even I who brought you together in the first place.'

He didn't bother to contradict her. She believed his relationship with Patricia had gone far beyond the limits it had and she wanted to be treated as a confidante, perhaps as consolation, perhaps as a gesture of secret spite against Dudley. If he took her into his confidence, she would remain his friend: if he didn't, and he couldn't, she would hate him.

She waited. When he didn't speak, her lips twisted. 'You're being very beastly.'

Emotionally, he thought, she was like a girl in her early 'teens. 'Hermione, I don't know where Pat is and only wish to God I did.'

'Why? What's wrong?'

He realised he'd revealed to much of his desperate fear. 'When I don't know where she is, I get worried,' he answered lamely.

'She'd have told *you* where she was going.'

'She hasn't told anyone. She wanted to be entirely on her own.'

'She's too considerate to act like that. But you won't tell me anything because you don't trust me. It ... it hurts most terribly.' She blinked rapidly and then tears began to spill down her coarsely grained cheeks.

He'd never seen such an ugly or pathetic sight as this ungainly, lumpy woman crying because she believed she was being excluded from the truth of a liaison.

There was a ring on the front door.

His relief was tremendous. 'I must go down and see who that is.'

She wiped her eyes with a handkerchief and stared up at him. 'Go on, then.' Her voice was now venomous. She knew no shades of grey in human relationships.

166

He left and went down the stairs to the front door. His mind was so occupied with the problem of Hermione that he was surprised to see French, accompanied by three other men, who between them carried two small, battered suitcases.

'Here's the warrant, empowering me to search this flat.' French handed over a double foolscap sheet of paper, folded into three, bearing on the outside the seal of the magistrates.

As Armitage stared at the warrant, not bothering to open it, there was a sound from the head of the stairs. Hermione, head held high, came down the stairs. She was wearing a valuable diamond and sapphire brooch, but on her it looked like costume jewellery.

When she reached the foot of the stairs she said to French: 'What are you doing here?'

'We've come to have a word with Mr. Armitage,' French answered easily.

She smiled at Armitage and he was shocked by the degree of malevolence, then she pushed her way through and out on to the pavement.

French closed the front door. 'Your co-operation will make our job easier and quicker,' he said briskly, to Armitage. He pointed beyond the stairs. 'Where does that door lead to?'

'The cellar,' answered Armitage dully, still shaken that Hermione could have been so obviously glad he was in some sort of trouble.

French detailed two of the men to go down to the cellar. Then he led the way upstairs. On the landing, stopping as if by chance by the patch of cleaned carpet, he said: 'Is there anything more you'd like to say regarding the present whereabouts of Mrs. Broadbent?'

Armitage shook his head.

French ordered the other two to search the rooms. They worked quickly, but neatly, checking drawers, cupboards and the clothes hanging in them, the soles and heels of shoes, beds, even the dirty linen in the basket. They were in the bathroom when one of the others came up from below and spoke to French. French turned to Armitage. 'Have you been digging down in the cellar?'

'I ... I can't remember,' muttered Armitage.

French shook his head, as if amazed by so stupid an answer. 'Four of the flagstones have recently been moved. Why have you had them up?'

Armitage didn't answer.

'Will you please come down with us.'

They all went down the two flights of stairs to the cellar. The overhead unshaded light, covered with dust, was giving off the characteristic odour now it was warmed up. A detective passed a torch across to French and he shone the beam on to the four flagstones that were pointed out to him. The earth between them had clearly been recently disturbed.

'Get the flagstones up,' ordered French, voice grim. At that moment he was certain that underneath they would find the body of Patricia Broadbent.

Within five minutes French and the others knew they'd been wrong. The earth had only been excavated down to a depth of about a foot, as evidenced by the compacted state of the yellow clay below this. French stood up and could not quite hide his surprise. 'Why did you dig that hole?'

A writer was supposed to have imagination, but Armitage's had gone on holiday. In the end he said weakly: 'I wanted to see what kind of soil the place was built on.'

French shrugged his shoulders. He turned and spoke to one of the younger detectives. 'D'you find anything else down here, Fred?'

'Nothing, sir, except the remains of a sandwich over there.' He pointed with the torch and the beam picked out two crusts.

French didn't bother to go over. 'All right, let's get back up top.'

When they'd finished searching the rooms they collected around the cleaned patch on the carpet. French said: 'We're going to carry out a test for blood.'

'You won't find any,' muttered Armitage, and wondered desperately whether his voice had sounded as false to the others as it had to himself.

One of the detectives switched on a torch and knelt down to shine the beam along the floorboards, gradually moving it away from the edge of the carpet. He quickly found something and French knelt by his side, then took the torch and slightly altered the angle at which it shone. He looked up. 'In artificial light, dried blood often has an appearance of glossy varnish. There's a patch of glossiness between at least two of the floorboards.'

A cold sweat prickled Armitage's forehead.

A detective took from one of the suitcases a small plastic container filled wth benzidine, two plastic tubes, some blotting paper, cotton wool, and a penknife. The blotting paper was damped with tap water whilst French sliced off a slither of wood from the edge of one floorboard. He put this on the dampened blotting paper, rolled it around, and poured a few drops of benzidine on to the blotting paper. In places it turned a light shade of blue. He stood up. 'Dig out half a dozen other slithers of wood, if you can find that many, and pack 'em in tubes.' He turned and spoke to Armitage. 'The initial test for blood has proved positive, but that's only presumptive and not necessarily specific. Further tests will be made at the police laboratory to make certain whether the stains on the wood are human blood and, if so, to group them. The carpet is only tacked down,

170

so we'll take it away for similar tests. Can you tell me what blood group you are?'

'It's ... it's on a medical card I have.'

'Will you go and find out what it is, please.'

Armitage went into his bedroom and took his wallet from his coat pocket. He returned to the passage. 'A two, Rhesus positive.'

French wrote down the classification in his notebook. 'Thank you.' He turned away and Armitage watched them pack several slithers of wood in dry blotting paper and the blotting paper in the test tubes. There was a label on each tube and French wrote on these the date, time, and place, and his initials. The others used a claw hammer to raise the carpet, which they rolled up and secured with string. With careful formality, French wrote out a receipt for the carpet and handed it to Armitage, then they left.

In terrified despair Armitage slammed his fist against the wall of the passage.

CHAPTER SEVENTEEN

The telephone rang as Armitage was pouring out the last of the whisky in the bottle.

'You've had a bleeding army of splits in.' Weir made it a question, a statement, and a vicious threat.

If that were possible, his fright increased

171

because the detectives were not long gone: the caller knew what was happening almost as it happened. 'They think I killed her and were looking for the body. They found traces of blood and went down to the cellar and discovered the flagstones had been moved. They thought I'd buried her there.'

Weir swore. His immediate idea was to make Patricia Broadbent ring her husband to say she was all right, but almost immediately he realised it was too late for that now—no call from her could explain the blood in the flat. If the detectives realised the blood hadn't come from Patricia Broadbent, they'd no longer accept the obvious solution which was her murder and they might have sufficient imagination to piece together what had really happened. So no matter what, they had to go on believing Armitage had murdered her. But what if she was a different blood group to Shocker's? ... How long could Armitage go without cracking now he was under pressure from both sides? ... 'If you don't want her learning how rough life can get, keep your trap tight shut whatever the splits do or say.'

'But I ...' The connection was cut. Armitage replaced the phone and then hurriedly swallowed down the whisky.

★   ★   ★

Weir paced the floor. He hated the bitch

beyond reason for not having said in time she wasn't married to Armitage. If she'd told them, they'd not have left the car around, they'd have put the pressure on the husband ...

He forced himself to accept that what had happened had happened. The police believed Armitage had murdered the missing woman, but had not yet sufficient evidence to arrest him. How long before they really put on the pressure and tore the flat apart—surely, when the blood on the floorboards and the carpet were grouped? Until they had those results, though, there'd be something of a lull whilst they checked out her bank balances, and so on. But the moment the blood group came through—if Shocker proved to have been of a different group—they were going to wonder whose blood that had been ...

So how long had he? Since the introduction of the breathalyser, all forensic laboratories had been buried under work, but this test would be priority. The results could even be through before the week-end.

Had he been a complete realist, his summing-up of the situation would have meant the end of the job. The risks had become too great. But now he'd assessed the position, he carefully ignored the logical conclusion.

Why shouldn't they move before the weekend? Bring in two extra men, as well as

173

Chiver Hyman who was taking the place of the dead Shocker, promise everyone the earth and the bloody planets as well if they worked fast enough. Burner could talk about all the time he needed, but that was only insurance. Put him in front of the door and he'd burn it in the time available. After the job they'd save more time by abandoning all the equipment. It was all cleanly nicked: it would tell the splits nothing.

He had to sell the job to the others. They knew things had taken a wrong turn and were getting scared. He'd tell them an extra consignment of money was due in. The thought of more money would make them forget all about the dangers of working to too close a time limit.

So it was still possible.

*   *   *

It was early dusk and Armitage was sitting in front of his typewriter, trying to make himself work, when the front-door bell rang. He shivered. That bell had come to mean trouble. It rang again. Reluctantly, he crossed to the window and looked down and could see a woman. Incredibly, it was several seconds before he identified Gwen.

He went down and opened the front door. She was brown and looking very fit, but there were new lines in her oval face. She said in a

174

low voice: 'Can I come in, George?'

He stood to one side, and it occurred to him that it must be days since he had last thought of her.

'Why are you looking at me like that . . .?' She put her fingers up to her right cheek, in a sad, lost gesture.

'How am I looking at you?' he asked.

'I . . . I don't really know.'

Nor did he. It was like meeting a friend from the long past and not knowing how to entertain her.

She again touched her cheek. She was wearing a light blue and yellow dress, with a sweeping · design in which the colours gradually intermingled and changed, simple but with the elegance of expensive quality. She had a small brooch that was new: a horse, picked out in diamonds. When she saw him looking so intently at it she hurriedly unclipped it and dropped it into her—new—crocodile-skin handbag. 'I . . . I'd thought . . . I hoped . . .' She began to cry.

He sighed, seemed about to touch her but didn't, then led the way upstairs and into the sitting-room. She sat down on the settee, opened her handbag and took out a handkerchief with which she wiped her eyes. He crossed to the table on which were the bottles and found there was some sherry left. 'Will you have a drink?'

She nodded.

He poured out the sherry and handed her the glass. She moved slightly, expecting him to sit next to her on the settee, but he went across to one of the armchairs. She drank, then opened her handbag and brought out a thin gold cigarette case, realised this was just one more visible sign of Fred Lett's wealth, and hastily took out a cigarette and dropped it back into the bag.

'How have things been?' he asked finally.

She shook her head. 'Not ... not too good. Fred changed.'

'How d'you mean, changed?'

'He became nasty and crude and tried to make me unhappy.'

'I could have told you that would happen, but you never stopped around long enough to ask me.' His voice was flat and without apparent rancour. 'His type get all their pleasure from pursuit, not capture.'

'If only ... If only things had been different and you could have made a little more money.'

'If only you could have learned to be grateful for what we'd got.'

'Can't you ...? Oh God! I know I've no right to expect you to understand what it was like always having to scrimp and save when everyone we knew had so much more money. To wear the same dress over and over again. To have a car that never started.'

'So you still think the important things are

material?'

She shook her head. 'I was trying to explain how things were.'

'Before you met Fred and were swept away by his gallant, sophisticated self? So different from me, a third-rate author?'

'Stop it!' she cried. 'You're being so cruel.'

He was being cruel!

'It wasn't a bit like I expected it to be.' Then she said something which showed how she had matured. 'It never could have been, could it?'

'No.'

'Will you believe me when I tell you I kept thinking of you? Imagining you trying to cope on your own, cooking, washing up ... Did you break much?'

'Not very much, really.'

'What about my blue plates?'

'I never used them.'

'Because you ... you thought I'd come back?' she asked, with sudden eagerness.

'No,' he answered flatly. 'I just reckoned that one day you'd want them sent on, along with the rest of your stuff.'

'Oh!' Wearily, she stood up.

'Was Fred ... ?' He stopped.

She guessed what his question was going to be. 'Was he good in bed? He's hopeless. At first he made a joke of it, saying he'd drunk too much, but it was always the same. That's when he began to get nasty—blaming me because he couldn't manage.'

So Fred wasn't an athlete in bed.

'Please, George, have me back? Even if only for a little?'

Tonight she could offer him the kind of scalding, uninhibited sex that could temporarily release a man from even his worst worries and fears. But if she stayed, she might learn about the robbery.

'I'm sorry,' he said.

She began to cry once more, but accepted his decision without argument. 'I won't bother you again.' Then she left, hurrying downstairs to get away from him.

CHAPTER EIGHTEEN

The lorry left the isolated farmhouse in the very early morning, hours before the two cars. Weir was awake to watch it off. Word from Ricard and Carver said nothing had blown up yet, so they were moving. Let the police laboratory waste another twelve hours in classifying the dried blood and they'd be too late. He shut his mind to the extra risk he was taking.

★　　　★　　　★

The day had been a busy and trying one for

Dudley Broadbent, trying because his secretary had been away ill and the girl who'd taken her place had made a complete mess of things, accepting two appointments for the same time on the same day and ruining three letters by gross misspellings.

He was glad to return home, even if Patricia were not yet back from her motoring holiday so that the house was empty: there was the television, a drink, and a cigar. And if he tried really hard, he did not think about what the police had told him or wonder what they were doing now.

When the front-door bell rang, suggesting company, he was annoyed because the television programme was one he especially liked. When he went through to the hall and opened the door and saw Hermione Grant his annoyance increased. She didn't wait for him to ask her in, but pushed past him to enter. She was rude, but not usually quite this rude, and when she stood in the middle of the hall, heavy legs akimbo, a twisted expression on her face and a queer look in her eyes, he had the unnerving thought that perhaps she'd gone mad. He looked past her at the telephone.

'So you've still not seen or heard anything of Patricia?' she said, her voice hoarser than usual.

He tried to exert some authority. 'My dear Hermione, what on earth...?'

'Haven't you guessed?'

'Guessed what?' he demanded testily.

'What the truth is ... I suppose you've got too old to be any good in bed?'

He blushed, as he hadn't blushed in years. 'Good God! How dare you say a thing like that?'

'You're not much good, either, at seeing what's right under your nose. You still can't even suggest a name for the bloke, can you?'

He stared at her, feeling a cold, icy numbness as in one sentence she stripped away all his careful self-pretence.

'I can tell you his name,' she said.

He stared at her and tried to speak twice before he mumbled: 'Brian?'

'Where would he suddenly find the guts to walk off with another man's wife?'

'Then ... You've got to tell me.'

She hesitated a long time before she said: 'George Armitage.'

He searched his memory and finally remembered the man. 'That writer fellow? But he hasn't got two farthings to rub together.'

'She wasn't after money, was she?'

He tried to disbelieve her, but her air of malignant triumph was too obvious. 'How do you know about him?'

'She used to come to me in order to pull the wool over your eyes and then go off from me to see him.'

Then Patricia's unfaithfulness was not even as a result of a sudden flash of passion, but came from a deliberate, drawn-out, sordid affair. He began to shiver. And she'd used this mistake of a woman as cover, knowing how he hated Hermione so that he'd never hear or check up on what was really happening.

'He's living in Ethington. Twenty-two, High Street.' Hermione watched him and slowly her triumph turned into bitter ashes as she understood that, pompous, vain and snobbish though he was, he'd truly loved Patricia and how he was hurt beyond recall. She gestured with her hands, as if trying desperately to explain and excuse, then turned and ran to the front door, her bumpy body bouncing, pulled open the door, and ran out.

He did not move until he heard the car drive away, then he shut the front door, returned to the sitting-room, and poured himself out a very large whisky. He drank. Now, he *had* to know. She *had* gone off with another man, a penniless, unsuccessful writer. He'd take Armitage to the divorce courts and teach him the cost of adultery . . . He finished the drink and poured himself another. Of course, a divorce could only mean bad publicity. The county families would very quickly desert a solicitor who got himself mixed up in a juicy scandal. Could he show true Christian magnanimity and take her back, knowing that another man had lain with her? Sex wasn't everything once a man had put a few years behind him. Age and wisdom taught one that the security of possessions was far more valuable than the temporary heat of sex. And looked at in a forgiving light it had to be admitted that she ran the house pretty much as he wanted it run.

Surely the thing to do was to talk to her, calmly and without rancour, and tell her that provided she realised and admitted the extent of her stupidity, he would forget and forgive and have her back. Of course, at the same time, he'd put the fear of God into the writer fellow and frighten him off.

He poured himself a third drink. He'd act now. He'd drive into Ethington, face the author fellow, and bring Patricia back.

On the drive, during which he did once wonder if he might have had one whisky too many, he decided exactly what line he'd take with each of them. He rehearsed the words he'd use, altering some of them when he decided he was being just a little too lenient towards Armitage.

Number twenty-two was over a shop. This increased his sad disgust. Couldn't the man even choose a respectable place for his liaison?

He rang the bell and waited, rang it again.

A full two minutes passed. He pushed in the button for the third time and kept it pushed in. If they thought they'd escape him by the juvenile expedient of trying to make out they were not in, they were mistaken. Eventually, the door was half opened, and Armitage, appearing strained, as well he might, looked out. 'What do you want?'

He could no longer stay calm. 'What the devil do you think I want? I wish to speak to Patricia.'

'I'm sorry, Dudley, she isn't here and hasn't been for days.'

'Would you mind not using my Christian name any longer? ... Please don't lie. I've been told on unimpeachable authority that my wife is here.'

'She isn't.'

'I insist on coming in to see her.'

'You can't come in.'

'Don't,' he said, with considerable dignity, 'be utterly ridiculous. He pushed the door more fully open and went inside. The door was slammed shut. He was aware of the figure of a man, only very hazily perceived, and then something hit his head with violent force. He tried to cry out, as he collapsed, but more blows landed on his head, rocketing him into unconsciousness.

CHAPTER NINETEEN

Weir looked away from Sails Fegan, one of the two extra muscle hands they'd taken on, and stared down at the unconscious man and thought that luck was finally riding with them. A man forced his way into the flat so that he had to be dealt with and he turned out to be the woman's husband.

'Are you sure the old fool was only trying to speak to his wife?'

Sickened by the sight of Broadbent's bloody head, Armitage answered hoarsely: 'That's what he said.' Weir frightened him sick because of his obvious, twisted viciousness. Like Patricia, though, he should have been far more frightened because Weir was not bothering to wear a hood.

When a man set out to find his wife, decided Weir, no one was going to be surprised when he didn't return too soon.

'Lofty,' said Fegan hurriedly, ''e just came busting in and we couldn't stop 'im.' He was a tall, broad-shouldered man and had used so much force that the cosh, made from canvas and sand, had burst.

'Drag the stupid bastard upstairs.'

'But he needs a doctor,' said Armitage.

'Are you crazy?' demanded Weir, before leaving them and going down into the cellar to see how the tunnel was progressing.

★   ★   ★

They'd tunnelled eight feet from the cellar wall and, after a final check with the plan, Weir crawled along the tunnel, lay down on his back, and began to use the ribbed cold chisel and a padded hammer. They could probably have safely used a power tool, but he refused to take further risks.

The job was difficult, painful, and uncomfortable, because flakes of concrete and the dust kept falling down on his face. But once again, luck was with them. The conduit had been laid lower in the concrete than the plans had specified so that he reached it sooner than expected. He cut the heavy pipe with a specially made tool, which he could use one-handed.

Hyman took Weir's place at the end of the tunnel. He had with him a compass, very heavily insulated wire cutters, and two rolls of insulated tape. He separated the mass of wires and was able to gain enough slack on each set to give fairly reasonable working conditions. The compass showed which of the outgoing small wires was carrying current: all these, he cross-contacted. Wires not carrying current, he cut. All alarms leading through the conduit had been immobilised. He cut through the outer cover of the mains lead-in to expose the three inner wires and separated these as far as was possible. Satisfied he was ready, he called out to go ahead.

Up top, everything was prepared for a critical exercise in timing. When the ingoing mains were cut the TV camera would cease to work, so that this must be done immediately after a P.C. had made a routine inspection of the screen and Dunder had the maximum time in which to set up the fake shot of the strong-room door.

They'd broken through from one of the upstairs bedrooms into the office above the bank and now Farnes cut through the wall between the office stairs and the bank. It was one of the more dangerous moments because there might just have been an additional system of alarms to those on the plans, with vibration sensors set in this wall. But all remained peaceful inside and outside.

They climbed through the hole into the bank and Beaver, the second new member of the mob, brought with him the very long, heavy electrical lead whose other end was plugged into the power supply in the flat. It proved to be an eerie experience for all of them. Through the tall glass windows they could see the street and even as the last of them entered, three people walked along the near pavement seemingly staring straight at them as they passed.

Initially, Carver was detailed to keep watch

186

through the window while the rest of them went past the manager's office to the stairs down to the vault. There was a door at the foot of the stairs and Weir opened it. Opposite, illuminated by bright overhead lights, was the huge strong-room door, metallic coloured, convex and ribbed, with massive red control wheel and a yellow panel above, in which were the time controls. The metal surround stretched from floor to ceiling and four feet either side of the strong-room door the plan told them that hidden steel 'fingers' stretched out another four feet into the concrete.

Weir stared at the door for several seconds, then jerked his gaze away and up to his right. High up was a TV camera on a tripod built out from the wall. 'Lou,' he said, and instinctively he kept his voice low.

Dunder put down his equipment or passed it across to others to hold and come past Ricard.

Weir pointed to the camera.

After a short while, Dunder said: 'O.K., Lofty. No trouble.'

They waited, nervous, even frightened by the camera.

Word came through that a P.C. had checked the screen and moved on. Weir gave the orders to cut the electricity and within thirty seconds the message reached Hyman. Very soon after that, all the lights went out.

Powerful torches were switched on. They moved quickly, each man knowing exactly what to do. Dunder went over to the wall, unplugged and unlocked the camera, took it down, and examined it. Beaver paid out the long power cable and fitted a multi-head socket and then he and Ricard fixed up two portable searchlights so that the vault was once more sharply illuminated.

Dunder worked quickly and confidently. He set up his camera, checked the lighting and had one of the portable searchlights altered, then shot a two minute take of the door. He spliced the tape so that it became continuous running, put it through a viewer to make certain all was well, then plugged in the camera and transmitted the take. 'O.K.,' he said. But it would not be until a patrolling constable looked at the screen above that they could be certain Dunder was right.

They split up. Farnes, Ricard, Carver, Gates, Hyman, and Fegan began the back-breaking job of carrying the gas bottles from the flat down to the vault while Aaron checked that all windows in the bank were shut so that the distinctive smell of the oxy-acetylene burner wouldn't escape the building at street level and then assembled the high-speed burner with special nozzles that allowed the consumption of oxygen to rise to ten thousand gallons an hour.

Above, in the main area of the bank,
188

Dunder watched a constable approach. The P.C. stopped and lit a cigarette, using the palm of his hand to hide it, then lifted the flap and studied the TV screen. He lowered the flap and walked on, clearly satisfied by what he'd seen.

*　　　*　　　*

Aaron switched off the gas and the flame died. He lifted the visor and used his forearm to wipe away the copious sweat from forehead and cheeks.

Weir came forward. He spoke thickly, because of the atmosphere. 'What's up, Burner?'

'There ain't nothing the matter 'cept I've sweated myself dry and need a drink and a break.' He left, to go up to the manager's office where the provisions were laid out.

Weir stared at the vault door. Aaron was trying to burn out a rough circle some two feet in diameter and along part of the circumference he had managed to break through the outer skin of metal, but elsewhere the metal appeared to have been no more than darkened.

'When Aaron returned, Weir said: 'You've not got far.'

'The door's good,' said Aaron shortly.

'But you'll get through?'

'I don't know yet.' He put on the helmet,

picked up the burner, re-lit the gas, pulled down the visor, fed in the oxygen, and resumed burning. The door was very good, but if it was humanly possible he was going to show it wasn't quite good enough.

CHAPTER TWENTY

Overcoming the heat, the weakening effects of dehydration, the choking atmosphere, Aaron worked on. It was going to be touch-and-go. If the door had been just a little stronger, even one more thickness of copper plate reinforced with manganese steel, he wouldn't have stood a chance in the time available, but as it was...

The pile of empty gas bottles was growing too rapidly. There was now the chance they would run out of oxygen.

*　　　*　　　*

Aaron completed the burning at ten past six. He tried to kick out the blackened, jagged central mass of metal, but was so weakened that the force of the kick sent him backwards and he collapsed to the floor. Farnes went past him and with several heavy blows knocked out the centre.

Inside, in addition to a couple of filing

190

cabinets and a large collection of trunks and cases belonging to customers, there were a very large number of sealed khaki canvas sacks, each of which contained ten thousand pounds in various combinations of denominations either in new notes, green labels, or used notes, red labels.

They threw water on the twisted, melted steel of the door and at first this was flashed into steam by the residual heat, but gradually they reduced the temperature. Then they laid sodden sacks over the bottom half and Weir scrambled through, at the cost of a sharp burn and a deep scratch in the right leg.

The air was solid with fumes and he coughed and gagged, but the excitement of success helped him to forget all discomforts. The fortune was his.

★   ★   ★

From time to time during the night Armitage had dozed off, but far from resting him, these brief periods of sleep had left him feeling washed-out and he had a pounding headache. He stared across the sitting-room at Gates, who was the only one of the three guards he'd had who'd been willing to talk to him. 'What would happen if you didn't succeed?' he suddenly asked.

Gates said: 'We wouldn't be rich.'

'I mean, what would happen to Mrs.

191

Broadbent?'

'Aw! She'll be straight, no matter. Wouldn't make no difference to her.' Gates tried to cover up the uneasy embarrassment the question caused him.

'And she was all right the last time you saw her?'

'Yeah.'

'But all that screaming over the phone?'

'It didn't last.'

Armitage was silent for a while. The nightmare was beginning to end. 'Where will you let her go? I'd like to get to her as soon as she's free.'

'You poor, stupid sod,' thought Gates.

'D'you think someone'll drive her back down here?'

'Lofty'll say as to that.'

'Is he the big bloke with a face like a battle scene?'

'Lofty's the little bloke.'

Armitage spoke slowly and uneasily, as if saying something he wanted to keep hidden, yet for some reason felt compelled to put into words. 'He gives me the creeps—like a chap I met years ago, who ended up in jail for something. He looks queer, with that soft skin. It's funny how often the runts of the world are mentally twisted—maybe it's because . . .'

The door slammed open and Weir came in, followed by Farnes who had a length of manilla cord in one hand. Farnes walked round to come up behind Armitage. Gates, eager to clear out of the room before the garrotting, hurriedly stood up.

'What were you saying?' demanded Weir in a high, thin voice.

Armitage was shocked by the violent hatred evident in Weir's face and he pressed back in the chair as if he'd been physically threatened.

Farnes looped the cord between his hands and prepared to throw it over Armitage's head.

'Hold it,' ordered Weir.

Astonished, Farnes waited, with his hands held at waist height. Armitage had no idea that death was just behind him.

Weir stepped over the still unconscious Broadbent. 'What were you saying about small blokes like me? I look queer? Funny how the runts of the world are all twisted?'

Armitage gripped the arms of the chair.

Weir's voice dropped to its normal level and pitch. 'You've got a lot to learn,' he said slowly. Ostensibly, he was once more calm, as if this had been one of those occasions on which he could switch off his anger, but Farnes could judge that the anger had merely been carefully stored away. Weir said to Gates: 'Take him downstairs to the lorry. He's going along with us.'

Gates muttered to Armitage to get moving

and Armitage got up from the chair. His legs were trembling. He was about to say something to Weir when Gates grabbed hold of his arm and forced him out of the room.

Farnes coiled up the cord. 'Why ain't you doin' 'im in now, like you said?' he asked.

'Because I reckoned he could be useful on the journey in case a car gets stopped.'

It was so weak an explanation, Farnes wondered that Weir should have bothered to make it. The truth was obvious. Armitage wasn't going to be allowed to die easily: he'd called Lofty a twisted runt and Lofty was going to prove to him that such words came expensive. Farnes stared at Weir, annoyed that a man clever enough to organise this robbery should be stupid enough to worry what a bloke called him. But even now Farnes wouldn't argue beyond a certain point. He stuffed the cord in his pocket.

*   *   *

Dudley Broadbent regained consciousness and he became vaguely aware that something was terribly wrong, but couldn't make out what. Then the pain flooded his head and speared it with white-hot fingers of fire.

The pain continued, but he began to understand his need for help. He tried to call out, but was aware that he'd done no more than croak. He was a stubborn man. Instead

194

of giving in to the pain and letting it engulf him, he continued to fight it and eventually opened his eyes. He saw a ceiling and walls that pulsated with a savage white light. He hurriedly closed his eyes again. Then, later, he suddenly realised he'd seen a telephone.

He forced himself to move. Inch by inch, he dragged himself across the carpeted floor to the table on which stood the telephone. He tried to reach up, but only succeeded in knocking over the table: this, however, brought the telephone crashing to the floor. The numbers on the dial were blurry, but he remembered how to dial 999 even if one could not see.

The operator asked him which emergency service he wanted and he tried to speak but failed. The pain intensified and all his stubbornness and courage weren't sufficient to combat it any longer.

The exchange had recently suffered a number of false emergency calls and the operator was about to cut the connexion when she heard a clock chime. False calls almost invariably came from call boxes. She listened more intently and thought she could just catch the rasping hiss of someone breathing very heavily and unevenly. She called the supervisor and kept talking about anything, to keep the line open whilst the supervisor set about tracing the call.

French, hungry because he'd been called away from home just as his wife had been about to break two eggs into the frying pan, stared at the hole in the wall of the bedroom in Armitage's flat and he remembered. There had been Armitage, terribly nervous, apparently very guilty. There had been the four flagstones, in the cellar, recently disturbed and seemingly marking a grave never completed. There had been the dried blood, so obviously from a murdered Mrs. Broadbent...

He looked back in time and bitterly thought that even though it had seemed certain it was the murder of Mrs. Broadbent he'd been investigating, even though almost any other D.I. would have worked on the same assumption, he could have seen the truth if only he'd had the imagination to do so. He hated his own incompetence.

*   *   *

'It's a pity you didn't appreciate the possibility,' said Detective Superintendent Connell, newly down from county H.Q. A tall, broad, florid man, he had an air of brisk competency.

French said nothing and stared bleakly across the sitting-room of Armitage's flat.

Connell wouldn't have done, French knew. Connell was the perfect H.Q. detective, notably adept at public relations, but he hadn't the untamed imagination this would have needed.

'All right,' said Connell, in tones which suggested the criticism was now over and forgotten.

Connell wouldn't forget it, French knew. 'There's one point I think we ought to concentrate on, sir. The fact they've taken Armitage with them and not murdered him here.'

'How can that be important? They'll just kill him somewhere else and dump his body.'

'Why go to all that trouble? His dead body could have told us nothing. The logical thing to do was to kill Armitage here. I think it could be vital to understand why they've acted illogically.'

'Perhaps.' Connell's tone of voice meant perhaps not. 'But right now I want this flat and the bank turned over inch by inch.'

French persisted. 'Suppose the answer's vital to saving Mrs. Broadbent?'

'You keep talking about logical and illogical. It's logical to presume she's dead by now. In any case, French, if she is still alive then the only way of saving her is to identify the mob immediately. That's why I want every man working flat out searching for traces.'

197

No sitting back, thought French, and 'wasting time', wondering, thinking, imagining, trying to understand the psychology of the villains. Connell was probably right. Certainly that was how the book would have it done. First, search for traces. No crime had ever been committed without traces being left. The difficulty was always in identifying them.

'Have you alerted all forces?' asked Connell. 'And requested information on all the burning equipment and TV gear?'

'Numbers and other identifying marks have been circulated by Telex.'

'Records?'

'I've been on to county and Metropolitan Records and asked for the names of all possibles for this job.'

'Every single man on the list is to be checked right out. How's Dabs getting on?'

'As fast as he can and two supports are on their way down from county.'

'With a mob this slick, there won't be any prints, but...' Connell shrugged his shoulders. The professionalism of crime was something they'd had to learn to live with. 'Beat constables?'

'They've all been recalled to the station and are being questioned with special reference to parked vans and lorries.'

'Are the numbers of the stolen notes going to help?'

'The bank manager says that these days they only keep the numbers of the twenties. There are too many fives and tens around to check them.'

'My God! When I was a kid, a fiver was a rarity . . . All right. Keep everyone at it.' He turned and left the room.

French stared blankly at the far wall. Did the fact that Armitage had been taken away suggest something odd about the psychology of one, or more, of the villains? Or was he now struggling to use too much imagination because when it had really mattered he had used too little?

A young D.C. came into the room. 'Found this, sir, down by the front door. Looks like it was part of the cosh they used on the old boy.' He held out a sheet of white cardboard on which was a small heap of sand and a piece of canvas which, from the way it had shredded, had begun to rot.

French put the sheet of cardboard on the small chairside table. The sand was fine, dry, and silvery, sea not builders' sand. The canvas had some lettering on it. He picked it up and carried it over to the window and the better light enabled him to make out the letters VEN. He cursed them for being so uninformative.

CHAPTER TWENTY-ONE

The P.C. was clearly nervous. He stood by the wall of the bank and fidgeted with the strap of his helmet, which he held under his left arm.

French called him across. 'All right. Let's have your report.'

Stony-faced, he spoke. He'd patrolled number eight beat, on the night turn, tried doors, looked in corners, shone his torch, checked everything, and at the end had signed his report N.T.R.—nothing to report. Which was a bad joke because millions of pounds had been stolen from his beat.

There was a pause. 'I looked at the TV screen regularly, sir ...' he began defensively.

French interrupted. 'We're not doubting you carried out your patrol.'

'Only that you'd got your eyes open,' snapped Connell. 'You should have noticed the TV picture had changed.' He stamped off.

French spoke with contrasting informality. 'Just have a good think back and see if there was anything which happened which didn't strike you then as being of any significance, but could now when you think about it in the light of the robbery.'

'I'm sorry, sir, but there's nothing. And about the TV picture...'

'It would have fooled anyone. What about the vans and lorries parked round your beat?'

The constable had already given the information to the duty sergeant back at the station. 'All known, sir.'

'Did you ever consciously look at the yard behind the flat so that you'd have seen the top of a van or lorry if it was high enough to be visible?'

'If anything had been visible, I think I'd have noticed it, simply because I've never seen anything parked in there at night before.'

'What about cars?'

The constable shrugged his shoulders. 'You know how it is, sir, with cars everywhere these days. Unless there's something special to fix one...'

'I know, but there was the one chance in a thousand you might have noticed something high-powered, parked close by the yard, like a Jag.'

The P.C. began to fiddle once more with the strap of his helmet. 'I did look over one Jaguar.'

'Why?'

'I was having a shufty round the car-park at the back—really, on account of Mrs. Broadbent's Morris having been found there. There was a this year's XJ 6 which hadn't got

201

a parking ticket. It just made me think that the richer they are, the meaner they come. Especially as there was a big Ford next door the same.'

Two large, fast cars, thought French. Could these have been the get-away cars? It would have been typical of the villains deliberately not to have paid the parking fee. 'What else did you notice about either of these cars?'

The constable shook his head. 'There wasn't nothing to notice.'

'Think back. Patrol the streets again. Did you flash your torch inside the Jag and see anything on the seats? You must have looked at the number plate to know it was the current year—what were the other numbers and letters?'

After a time the P.C. said: 'It's no good, sir.'

'Keep trying and if you remember anything get on to me fast.'

After the constable had gone, French walked to the nearest window and stared out at the inevitable crowd, attracted by the police activity. An intense sense of urgency gripped him. Yet what could he do now to help either Mrs. Broadbent or Armitage ...? But why hadn't Armitage been murdered in his flat? Why bother to take him off alive? Unless for some perverted reason? And this brought French full circle back to the desperate urgency.

He left the bank, through the hole in the wall, went up the stairs to the office above, then through the hole in the wall there to the bedroom of the flat. He lit a cigarette. Was there anything he'd overlooked? Was he clean missing some vital point? Next door, in the other bedroom, there was suddenly and incongruously a deep belly laugh from one of the searching detective constables.

This mob had been real professionals, with inside information that stretched right back to the murdered Healey. Real professionals would surely never have left Armitage entirely on his own after the first and abortive attempt to rob the bank? Even though they'd got Mrs. Broadbent, Armitage might risk her life or might blow his top, unable to take the pressure, and they'd have to know so that they didn't return to find half the county police waiting for them. Someone must have been around to watch. Yet the search of the flat on the Wednesday had shown that that someone hadn't been in the flat. So they must have kept watch from outside.

He left the bedroom, hurried up the short length of passage into the sitting-room, and stared through one of the windows. They'd have been somewhere opposite, within visual range of this flat. When the police called on Tuesday and Wednesday, word would have got back ... Had they killed Mrs. Broadbent then, but let Armitage think she was still alive?

He called and the two detectives came out of the first bedroom, where they'd almost finished their search. Connell, thought French, would create hell if he learned his D.I. had pulled men off the immediate jobs—but to hell with Connell. 'The mob must have had a look-out somewhere opposite. Get out and find it.'

The two detective constables left the flat.

*　　*　　*

One of the two detective constables who'd been searching for the look-out reported back to the D.I. 'The estate agent says the flat was let to Mr. Charles Barnes from the third of last month, rent a thousand a year, six months in advance.'

From what the other had told him, French had no doubts that this had been the look-out. No one legitimately rented a flat and paid a six months' advance and then didn't use the place normally: the beds weren't made up, with the exception of two blankets the bed linen was still in cleaner's plastic bags, there was a film of dust in most places but where there wasn't all surfaces had carefully been wiped clear of prints, the cutlery was still neatly stacked in half dozens as it had been for the inventory ... One might have thought the flat hadn't been occupied at all except that there'd been an electricity consumption of just over a hundred and fifty units.

The D.C. handed French a magazine. 'This is the only definite thing we've found. It had slipped down the side of the settee.'

French examined the high-quality pornographic photographic magazine. Such material was readily available in London or other major cities, but much more difficult to buy in somewhere like Ethington—though there were known suppliers on whom the police kept a general eye but did not raid unless there was good reason. This might have come from one of the local suppliers.

*　　　*　　　*

It was one-thirty and with most people at lunch Nestor seemed virtually deserted. It was a seaside town, catering for those on small budgets, and its season ran from June to September so that at other times it became a place of shuttered shops, stalls, and holiday camps. Only the sand, virtually untrodden, and the grey-green sea held any beauty.

D.C. Tendron went into the corner tobacconist and newsagent and the door bell pinged. The owner, Dickens, large, flabby, and with a slight lisp, came into the shop from the room beyond. Still chewing as he entered, he swallowed hastily when he recognised the D.C. 'Hullo, Mr. Tendron.'

Tendron handed over the magazine, in a large brown paper bag for decency's sake. 'Have a look at this and tell me if it's one of yours?'

Dickens brought out the magazine, studied the inside of the front cover, bringing it close to his face to check some nearly invisible pencil marks, and then nodded. It was a strange quirk of his to try never to admit verbally to selling pornographic material.

'Can you tell me when you sold it?'

Dickens scratched his head. He turned and pushed through bead curtains to the room behind.

The D.C. was hungry. He went over to one of the sweet counters and picked up a four-ounce bar of milk chocolate which he began to eat.

Dickens returned. 'They came in a fortnight back and I've only sold three copies.'

'You'll be going bankrupt soon if you don't improve trade,' said the D.C., through a mouthful of chocolate. 'So you sold three. Who to and never mind the regulars. I want to know about an oddball?'

Dickens fiddled with his nose. 'One of 'em I've never seen before.'

'So how would he know you sold this sort of crap?'

Dickens showed no resentment. 'He thumbed through *Playboy* and asked me if I'd something stronger. I brought this out.'

'Describe him.'

'He was about your age—maybe a year or two more. Had a long face, plenty of hair, and was tough-looking and loud-voiced. He was dressed smart.'

So far, thought Tendron, the description could fit almost any tearaway between the ages of twenty and thirty-five. 'What about height, colour of eyes, colour of hair, and physical peculiarities?'

Dickens rocked back on his heels and closed his puffy eyelids. 'There was something . . . something he said . . .' He opened his eyes. 'That's right. After he'd bought the mag, he asked for a paper to find out how his team had done. Spoke with a bit of an accent. Took him three papers to find one that listed the game.'

'What was his accent?'

'North.'

'What team was he on about?'

'Workington.'

'Rugby league, eh? Stuff for strong, sweaty men. Anything else?'

Dickens shook his head.

Tendron wrote in his notebook. 'Thanks, mate. By the way, I had a bar of chocolate, so what do I owe you?'

'Nothing,' replied Dickens sadly. 'Have it

on the house.'

★   ★   ★

D.C. Tendron reported the result of his questioning over the phone.

In his office, French began to doodle with a pencil. Fifteen minutes before, news had come through that the gas cylinders and burning equipment had been stolen from Carlisle. This man spoke with a northern accent. He'd been interested in how Workington had done. The sand from the cosh was sea sand. The piece of canvas had had the letters VEN on it and near Workington was Whitehaven. Everything pointed to the north-west coast of Cumberland. Or did it? The gas cylinders had been stolen from Carlisle. The gang might have stolen them or bought them from a middleman. If they'd stolen them, there was always the fifty-fifty chance they'd done so far away from their base of operations for obvious reasons. The man who'd bought the pornographic magazine had spoken with a 'northern' accent and was interested in how Workington had done. The police didn't know for certain—in the sense they couldn't prove—that the flat had been used as the look-out. They didn't know that the magazine had been bought by someone who'd been in the flat—it could have passed through a third person's hands. A 'northern' accent could mean anyone who was not from the south. The man was interested in Workington rugby team, but that didn't mean he must still live within their territory. If the man did come from near the Cumbrian coast, it didn't follow the mob did ... But it was odds on the flat had been used as a look-out. Would one of the look-outs have palled up with a local to the extent of buying or borrowing an expensive pornographic magazine? A Cumbrian accent was fairly certain to be identified as northern. A sharp interest in a rugby team tended to suggest a present territorial involvement with their fortunes rather than a past one. The leader of a mob always tended to recruit locally because then he personally knew the qualities of the people. Whitehaven and Workington were near an endless supply of sea sand ... But how many hundreds of miles of beaches were there round the British Isles? How many towns' names contained VEN? Newhaven, Milford Haven, Peacehaven ...

The scraps of information were of ambiguous nature and to say they irresistibly pointed to the coast of Cumberland as the home of the mob was to ignore all common sense and logic. And to go further and say that it was certain Armitage had not been killed because someone in the mob had a perverted wish to make Armitage suffer a great deal before he died, and that his aim was probably to be attained by killing Mrs. Broadbent in front of him, so that there *was* still time left in which to save them both . . . This was to become ludicrous. And to proceed from these assumptions to the assertion that travelling north towards Cumberland was one large van or lorry, a this year's Jaguar—could there be less proof of anything than that the Jaguar without a parking ticket had been one of the gang's get-away cars?—and a large Ford, that these cars would be heading for the coast, and that the geography of the area being what it was, with the mountains between motorway and coast, the three vehicles would travel one of the only two reasonable routes and therefore there was a chance of intercepting the Jaguar . . . Well, that was to become plain bloody silly.

So he was on to a hiding for nothing. And, in any case, action involving another police force would have to be initiated by the detective superintendent after obtaining permission from the assistant chief constable. Connell, rightly according to all the rules, wouldn't consider such action on this so-called evidence.

But suppose, just for once throw logic away and use sufficient wild imagination to suppose, that all the threads, ambiguous, fashioned out of sky-hooks, did all point together, northwards. Suppose that there was a chance of picking up some of the mob in the Jaguar whilst it was driving north, but that once the cars had arrived at their destination there was no chance at all of locating the mob in time to save Armitage and, if alive, Mrs. Broadbent . . .

He reached across for the telephone. He was probably committing professional suicide. But he had to live with his conscience.

CHAPTER TWENTY-TWO

Harcourt, driver of patrol car Charlie Fox One Zero, on the road between Penrith and Keswick, spoke with all the resentment of a man who'd been told by his wife that morning that she thought she was pregnant yet again. 'Look for a this year's Jaguar XJ 6. Colour not known, registration number not known. Perhaps in company with a large Ford, model, make, and colour not known . . . Do those silly bastards at H.Q. know anything?'

'Not much,' replied Jeans, the observer.

It was a relatively straight stretch of road, running along the crest of a hill, and cars were speeding until they caught sight of the white police Triumph.

'I'm telling you,' went on Harcourt, his voice thick with the flat Cumbrian accent of the middle hills, 'if they ran an I.Q. test on 'em, they'd call in a bunch of monkeys to take their place.'

'Something seems to be biting you hard today, Mike?' said Jeans.

Harcourt was not prepared to give the reason—with five children already, he was the butt of too many jokes. 'Listen. How many bloody Jaguars do they reckon are on the road?'

'Were you on the beer last night?'

'Me? Where d'you think I'd get that sort of money from?'

Ahead of them were two cars and two articulated lorries. The second lorry drew out to overtake the first, but clearly lacked the speed to get by very quickly.

'What's he think he's doing?' demanded Harcourt. 'We'll just stop that lad and tell him a few facts of life.' He started the flashers and drew out.

It was the lorry-driver's bad luck, thought Jeans, to get Mike on one of his bad days. Mike had a hell of a temper. He half turned as they reached the two cars and noticed the leading one was a green Jaguar XJ6. 'There's a new Jag.'

'To hell with that. I want a word with the driver of that goddamn lorry.'

Jeans was interested to note that both

driver and front passenger of the Jaguar stared stolidly ahead. This was odd. The occupants of a vehicle overtaken by a police car usually looked across from interest or because of a guilty conscience. 'I reckon we might usefully have a chat with the blokes in that Jag.'

'After I've told the lorry-driver a thing or two!'

They stopped the lorry and the other vehicles went by. The driver turned out to be so meek and mild and apologetic that Harcourt felt frustrated. As he returned to the police Triumph, he said: 'You want to stop some bastards in a Jaguar? Come on, then.' He stuck out his chin.

★　　　★　　　★

'There's that cop car again,' said Carver, looking through the back window.

'Stop fretting,' advised Gates. He checked his speed.

Dunder, in the back, said: ''E's flashing 'is lights.'

Gates checked the speed again. 'We're in the clear.'

'Then why's 'e flashing us?' demanded Carver roughly.

'Cool it, Angel. So 'e wants a chat.' The police Triumph drew alongside and the observer motioned to them to pull in. Gates braked. 'Take it gentle,' he warned.

Carver swung round in his seat and faced Armitage. 'You remember. Lofty's in the van and if we don't get back sharp, Lofty's going to teach your bit of nookey a lot.'

''E knows the score,' muttered Gates, as he stopped the car. He wound down his window.

Harcourt and Jeans left the Triumph and walked back to the Jaguar.

'Sorry to bother you,' said Jeans, speaking pleasantly.

'Aw, no bother,' replied Gates. 'Something up, then?'

'We've been asked to check on all new Jaguars—been a bit of trouble somewhere. Is this one yours?'

'That's right.'

'May I see your driving licence and insurance certificate?'

'Sure. Always provided I've got 'em with me.' Gates, knowing that the expertly forged papers were in his inside coat pocket, spoke with just the right degree of nonchalance. He took from his wallet a driving licence and insurance certificate, both in the name of Grieves.

Jeans checked the papers and handed them back. 'That's fine, then.'

'You had me worried I was doing seventy-one,' joked Gates.

'Never trouble anyone until they're doing the ton. Been down south, have you?'

'Just a quick look at the sights, yeah.'

Jeans casually glanced at the other occupants of the car and spoke to Carver. 'I reckon we've talked before?' It was an idle question, showing casual interest and without special significance. He accepted them as legitimate and intended to do no more than have a quick look in the boot before waving them on.

A man of more experience than Carver would have made some equally casual remark and that would have been that. But Carver was nervous and a braggart. 'We don't know each other, mate. I'm particular.'

Harcourt came forward, hands on hips, an aggressive expression on his face. 'Hullo. What have we turned up? A joker?'

Afraid of where the other's temper might lead them, Jeans said: 'Forget it, Mike.'

Harcourt ignored the observer and stared down at Carver. 'Would you like to tell us your name?' Then he looked past Carver into the back of the car and saw that one man—Armitage—was sweating. 'I reckon it'd be a good idea if you all got out of the car so as we could have a closer look at you.'

Gates spoke in a very conciliatory voice. 'I'm sure Jack didn't mean nothing...'

'It'll be better if you leave him to tell us.'

Carver, belatedly trying to repair the damage he'd caused, stepped out of the car. The others didn't move and for the moment

215

Harcourt didn't press them.

'What's your name?' asked Harcourt.

'Wright,' replied Carver.

'What Wright?'

'Albert Wright.'

'Is that all?'

'Yeah.'

'Then just explain something. Why did your mate call you Jack?'

The observer, still on the other side of the car, said suddenly: 'I've put some facts to the face. The last time I saw his mug, he'd been nicked for helping out with a heavy mob.'

Escape was their only hope now and Carver belted Harcourt in the stomach. Harcourt grunted explosively and half doubled-up. Gates began to jump out of the car, but Jeans shut the door on him and caught his knee, pinning it against the sill and knocking him back and sideways so that his head crashed against the roof of the car. Harcourt was about as tough as he looked. He overcame the blow to his stomach and brought his knee up into Carver's groin in time to make Carver mistime a second blow. Carver collapsed to the grass verge, clutching himself. Harcourt whirled round for the next fight, but Dunder was standing very still by the side of the car, Gates was only just recovering his senses, and Armitage hadn't moved.

'Sit down on the grass so as we can be certain you're going to be all nice and

216

peaceful,' said Harcourt, now in good humour.

Carver already lay on the grass. Dunder hurried to sit down beside him, Gates limped round and then virtually collapsed.

Harcourt went back to the car and spoke to Armitage through the open front doorway. 'If it wouldn't be troubling you too much, mate?'

Armitage didn't move.

Harcourt's voice quickened. 'Get out of the bloody car before I pull you out.'

Armitage said wildly: 'You blind fool!'

Harcourt's good humour finally slipped. 'All right, if that's the way you want things...'

'You've just killed her.'

★　　★　　★

Over the car's radio, H.Q. had confirmed all that Armitage had said. Harcourt and Jeans were shocked at the situation they had precipitated, yet uncertain how it could have been avoided. Both policemen hoped C.I.D. would soon be along to take over and remove the job from their shoulders.

'You've got to let us go,' said Armitage wildly. 'I've told you what they'll do to her if you don't.'

Harcourt moved, to stand over Carver. 'Where is she?'

217

Carver stared into space.

'I'll give you to just three to start talking.'

'And then what?' sneered Carver. 'And I don't know nothing about that bit of tit he's on and on about.'

Harcourt shifted his weight, as if about to kick.

'You so much as touch me,' shouted Carver, 'and my mouthpiece'll fix you, good and proper.'

Jeans looked warningly at Harcourt. Whatever their feelings, wherever their sympathies lay, they dare not touch these men now.

'Make 'em talk,' demanded Armitage.

Harcourt jammed his massive fists into the pockets of his trousers.

'If you won't, I will.'

'Sorry,' said Jeans, speaking brusquely to conceal his emotions.

'Didn't you hear what they're going to do to her?'

'Yes, but...'

'But? Suppose it was your wife?'

Jeans had already supposed that. If his wife were involved, he'd have smashed these men into a bleeding pulp to make them talk. Yet, with bitter irony, if Armitage tried to touch them, he and Harcourt would have to restrain him.

'They're going to rape her and...'

'She'll love it all,' jeered Carver.

Armitage flinched.

Gates spoke thickly. 'I'll tell you where she is.'

CHAPTER TWENTY-THREE

As he drove the Jaguar up the narrow lane, bordered by drystone walls, with the hills visible whenever the rolling cumulus didn't obscure the moon, Armitage could feel his stomach churning and he thought he'd either be sick or have to stop the car and dive behind one of the walls.

'Take it easy,' said the detective sergeant by his side.

How in the name of hell could he?

The headlight of the car—only the one was working: they'd carefully driven the Jaguar into a concrete bollard to make it seem it had been in a crash—showed them the stone walls were now in considerable disrepair. An old apple tree, gnarled, leaned over the road. Above the humming of the engine, they heard the mournful hoot of a long-eared owl.

'Remember,' said the detective sergeant, 'you tell whoever comes to the door that you had an accident and two of the blokes are in hospital, but the third one's with you. Give him a name. How did they call Gates?'

'Alf.'

'You say Alf's with you and you need help to get him inside. If you catch sight of Lofty Weir and he's not in a hurry to come out, just tell him he looks like a Hottentot pygmy. From all accounts, that'll get him out of the house like a dose of salts.' The detective sergeant chuckled.

A rabbit scuttled out into the road and became hypnotised by the car's headlight. Armitage only just missed it. They rounded a corner and saw a rotting gate and beyond that an overgrown track which ended in front of a rectangular, stone-built house.

One of the detectives in the back sent out a message over the portable radio to say they were approaching the house. Reinforcements would now be sent on their way.

'All right,' said the detective sergeant, 'leap to it.' He wriggled down as far as he could out of sight. In the back, one of the D.C.s dropped to the floor and the other, with a bandage tied round his head, huddled in the corner.

They drew up, on weed-filled gravel, in front of the house and as Armitage switched off the headlight he saw someone look out of the right-hand upstairs window.

'And the best of British luck to one and all!' murmured the detective sergeant.

Armitage opened the driving door and the interior light went on. From the house, only the man in the back, huddled in the corner,

220

was visible. Armitage stepped out and slammed the door shut. On the house, the outside light above the door was switched on.

'What happened?' demanded a voice he recognised as Weir's, from the upstairs bedroom.

'There ... there's been an accident.' Tension and fright made his voice shake and unwittingly it added veracity to his words. 'Alf was driving and there must have been a spring because the road was suddenly wet and he skidded and hit a wall. The others had to be taken off to hospital, but Alf wasn't bad enough. The police don't suspect a thing.'

Weir studied the car. 'It don't look to have been in a bad crash.'

'It's much worse than it looks. It was a job to get here but I had to make certain nothing's happened to Patricia.'

The window was shut.

Armitage waited by the car, cold sweat beading his body and head.

The front door opened and Weir came out, followed by Farnes. It was immediately obvious that, with some animal-like sixth sense, Weir suspected a danger, yet couldn't be certain why. He walked up to the front of the Jaguar. 'This hasn't been in any bad crash.'

'But I tell you, I was only just able to drive it here.'

'What d'you mean? The wheels ain't

touched. What's going on...?'

The car doors were flung open and the detectives spilled out. Even though this was so totally unexpected, Farnes's reactions were so quick that he countered a blow from the nearer D.C. and landed one in return which dropped the detective to the ground, where he lay twitching, grabbing at his stomach. Farnes kicked out at the detective sergeant and although he didn't land squarely, he still sent the other staggering backwards. Weir had a flick knife with which he faced the second D.C.

They'd given Armitage a truncheon, purely as a morale booster. He reached inside his coat, dragged it from the waist of his trousers, and tried to strike Farnes. Farnes side-stepped easily and hit Armitage high up on the shoulder with a blow that sent him backwards. The detective sergeant, showing great courage, threw himself at Farnes and landed a karate blow that seemed to leave Farnes unhurt and Farnes gained a vicious hold on the other's head and dug in his thumbs to try to force the eyeballs out of their sockets. Armitage came back again and swung the truncheon and by luck it caught Farnes's nose and broke it, making him bellow from the sudden agony. The detective sergeant drove home a right well below the belt and Farnes gasped, gagged, and collapsed.

The detective sergeant went to help the D.C. facing Weir, but Weir was flicking the knife from hand to hand, with expert timing, making it impossible for them to close. Armitage came up behind and slammed down the truncheon on Weir's head. The D.C. jumped in and grabbed both Weir's hands and twisted and Weir, in his weakened state, didn't have the strength to resist. The knife fell and the D.C. released Weir.

Suddenly, Armitage knew a blood-lust. He slammed the truncheon into Weir's face, kneed him, heard the high-pitched scream with a pleasure almost sexual, hit him again to knock him to the ground, and kicked him.

The detective sergeant dragged him away and sanity returned. They ran into the house and as the D.C. slammed open the front door, they heard the rising note of an approaching car. Aaron, Ricard, Hyman, Beaver, and Fegan stood in a tight bunch in the hall. The detective sergeant said, with harsh confidence: 'Just keep quite still and you won't get hurt.'

Aaron and Hyman made it clear they weren't going to start anything. Beaver and Fegan were undecided, Ricard obviously wanted to fight but found himself on his own.

'Where have you got her?' Armitage shouted.

They stared at him, but no one answered. There were stairs at the back of the hall and he ran up these, automatically assuming they'd have imprisoned her upstairs. There was a small, square landing and to the right of this was a short passage in which stood Bert Smith, a knife in his hand. They heard the oncoming car brake to a tyre-squealing halt and the noise of a number of men jumping out and a shouted string of commands. Smith dropped the knife to the floor.

Armitage rushed past Smith, found the door behind him unlocked, slammed it open, and went in. Patricia lay on the bed, a sheet covering her. She stared at him for several seconds, as the previous wild hope grew into certainty, then she began to cry. He took her into his arms and discovered the little clothing she wore was torn to ribbons. Her flesh was bruised. When he hoarsely asked her what they'd done to her, she cried more wildly, but wouldn't answer.

★   ★   ★

It was June. Glorious, flaming June. Only the sky was a dirty grey and it was raining. In the sitting-room of his flat Armitage stared out at the wet, dismal scene for a time, then he turned. 'But you can't,' he said vehemently.

'Please, George, try and understand.' Patricia spoke entreatingly. There were new lines in her face to mark the suffering she had known.

'But I ... I can't understand how you can go back to Dudley.'

'Because he's so ill, that's why. The doctors say it's still touch-and-go.'

'He can afford to have trained nurses look after him.'

'George, you're forgetting—he's my husband.'

'You don't love him.'

She looked away, biting her lower lip.

'Have you forgotten all you said, when I found you in that room?'

'How ... how could I?'

'Leave him, Pat. Grab some happiness...'

'I couldn't be happy, knowing that I'd deserted him when he most needed me.'

'You can't be expected to sacrifice everything for him. And what sort of loyalty did he show you? Hermione had only to tell him you were with me and he was convinced you were committing adultery.'

'He'd every reason to think that. I'd been seeing you clandestinely. If I hadn't visited you when I shouldn't, he'd never have had to come to this flat to try and find me and he wouldn't have been so terribly hurt. Don't you see, George, every time I look at him and realise what he's been reduced to, physically and mentally, I have to know that I'm responsible.'

'You're suffering a totally unnecessary sense of guilt.'

225

e spoke despairingly. 'I can't leave him. ... not while he's still alive.'

He was forced to accept the fact that no words of his would make her alter her mind. Only Dudley's death could release her from her self-imposed expiation. He returned from the window and slumped down in one of the armchairs. Gwen and he, Patricia and Dudley, all bystanders, had had their lives shattered. The police said that the man buried under the new motorway had been murdered by the gang and another man had been killed in a car crash because of them. One of the gang had died in the flat. All this suffering as the result of one crime and perhaps more that no one yet knew about. What was it that Hermione had once said? He didn't write realistically about violence because he didn't know its true colour. He knew that now. But did this new knowledge mean that from now on his writing would improve so dramatically that every one of his books would be a best-seller? He doubted it.

Photoset, printed and bound in Great Britain by REDWOOD PRESS LIMITED, Melksham, Wiltshire